The
Troublemaker

NEW YORK TIMES BESTSELLING AUTHOR
CLAIRE CONTRERAS

The Troublemaker

Chapter One

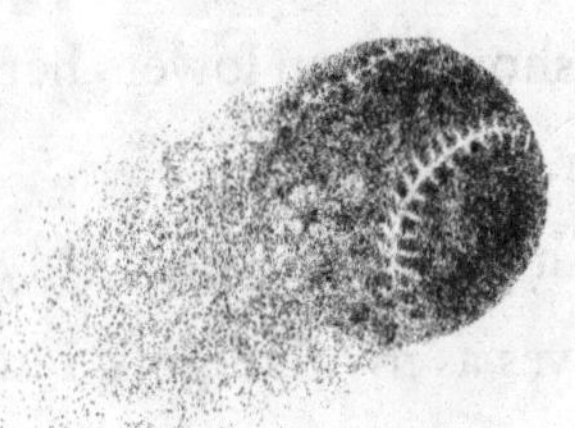

THE HUSHED CHATTER CARRIES THROUGH THE CAMPUS, SPILLING over to the county beyond. Athletes are being arrested and charged. Evidentially, there's been a long-running drug ring that's just now being exposed. If the extra police cars parked around campus hadn't given it away, the FBI jackets running around surely would have. I locate my phone in my bag and recheck the news to find that two more athletes have been arrested. I stop breathing as I scroll, bracing myself to see if they've given any names. It's not like I know every single athlete in town, but I know two who I can only hope aren't involved in this. Since the news hasn't revealed names, I call my sister. She answers on the first ring.

"This is insane," she says.

"I know." I bite my lip. "Have you heard from Mitch or Mav?"

"Yeah, they're shook."

"But not involved, right?" I brace for the answer.

"No," my sister shouts, then lowers her voice. "God, no. They would never."

"Yeah, I know, but you never know." My words are as at odds with themselves as my thoughts. I just can't grasp any of this.

"Are you on campus now?"

"Yeah." I sidestep a bike rider and start walking on the grass. "Are you house touring today?"

"Yep." She sighs. "This is exhausting. I've already seen three properties, and they're all so beautiful, but I don't even know what I'm looking for anymore, you know? Do I want an apartment so I don't have to deal with a yard, or do I want a house?"

"Well, that depends. Are you going to have kids any time soon?"

"No."

"Do you and Jagger want to stay in Charlotte even after his contract with the Panthers is made?"

"I don't know. I mean, we love it here, but I don't know.

I guess it depends on whether or not he retires as soon as he says he wants to retire."

"I don't see how he wouldn't after he's made such a big deal about it," I say, half joking, but it's true.

"Tell me about it," Jo mumbles with a laugh.

My soon-to-be brother-in-law, who also happens to be my ex's brother, has been making a big deal out of this forever. He signed an NFL contract with the Panthers but stated that he would only play for three years from the get-go. The agreement is so good that I can't imagine ever living in a reality where I'd pass up that kind of money, but he says he knows what's best for him, his brain, and his body. I guess I can joke about it since I'm not the one taking a beating every time my cleats hit the turf. I respect him for knowing when to walk away, and I'm grateful he chose Charlotte, which is only a couple of hours away from me, so I can visit my sister any time I want.

"I have to go. I just pulled up to a mansion," she says. "This is a definite no. I'd have to have a cleaning lady here every week to maintain this number of windows."

"God, Jo. I really can't imagine having such a hard life."

"Shut up, smartass." She laughs. "Keep me posted on your internship stuff, and let me know if anyone we know gets arrested. Have you checked on Bobby or Dylan?"

"No."

"Maybe you should."

"You think they'd sell drugs?" My eyes widen. I stop walking when I get to the school paper building, where I'm taking my last journalism class.

"I don't know. Would they?" She pauses. "I have to go. Love you."

I drop my phone back into my bag and think about that as I walk into the building. I don't even know how to categorize Dylan's and my relationship. A relationship isn't one way, that's for sure. We went on three casual dates, which ended without any significant hooking up. We kissed twice, the second leading to light petting over clothes. I'd been the one to make a move to stop it from going further. He was my ex-boyfriend's teammate, and that made things weird for me. Not that Mitchell was someone I'd get back together with or anything, but I didn't know if they'd talk in the locker room about me, and the idea was making me doubt myself and my actions too much, so that was where things died down.

After that, our frequent texts became once-in-a-blue moon texts. So, did I think he'd sell drugs? I wasn't sure. Would a white, handsome, athletic, twenty-three-year-old from a well-to-do family need a side hustle? It was something I couldn't wrap my head around. I was a brown, beautiful, athletic, twenty-two-year-old from a well-to-do family, and I didn't even need a main hustle. I'd gotten a job at a coffee shop near campus, mostly because I wanted to buy myself some overpriced designer sneakers I'd seen, loved, and couldn't ask my parents to buy me without it being my birthday. Was I spoiled? Absolutely. Was I a brat? No way. I didn't take anything I had for granted.

"Nice to have you in here, Misty Canó," Professor Eugene Madison calls out when I step into the large meeting room.

"Always a pleasure, Professor." I shoot him a smile as I take a seat beside Soleil.

She beams me a smile when she looks over at me. We've been in most of the same classes since we started here and hit it off rather quickly. Soleil is an international student from France, which I think is the coolest thing ever. I couldn't imagine leaving the country to study abroad, but now I can't imagine Soleil going when this semester is over.

"We're discussing what everyone is going to write about for their final project," Professor Madison says, filling me in. "This is in conjunction with what you're already writing for the school paper."

"How much of the grade will rest on this project?" I ask.

"All of it."

"All of it?" I blink, looking around at my seven peers, who look as nervous as I feel.

"It gets better," Professor Madison says, with way too much excitement in his tone. "They will be entered in a contest, and the winner will be published in a sports journal."

"What?" My jaw drops. I look at Soleil, who's nodding enthusiastically. "That's huge."

"The seven of you have been assigned to a specific magazine, journal, or newspaper. You'll find the name written inside the envelope set in front of you. We'll get to those later."

"Aw, come on," Ricky says. "You know we're dying to know."

"Yes, but first, I think we need to discuss the elephant in the room." Professor Madison shoots him a look. "We've all seen the FBI running around campus. They're also all over the UNC campus—"

"Who cares?" one of the guys says, making a few people laugh.

"We should all care." Professor Madison shoots them a look. "We may have a rivalry, but both of our schools are facing serious allegations. That's why we're partnering up with the UNC newspaper to highlight each other's athletes, the ones not involved in these crimes, the ones who will take a fall for something they didn't commit."

"What does that mean?" Soleil asks beside me.

"It means we include them in our assignments," Professor Madison says. "You may open your envelopes now. I want everyone to come up with a subject for their assignments by Friday."

We all open our envelopes. Ricky Pope fist-bumps the air and shouts, "ESPN!" The rest of us glower at him as we turn our papers over because he already took the one we all wanted. My paper reads Cruz Media. It's Milly and Roberto Cruz's company. Is it a coincidence that I was chosen to intern at my parents' friends' and my ex-boyfriend's company, or is this a setup? I don't want my peers to know the connection, so after class, when everyone else goes back to their workspaces, since we all work for the newspaper, I decide to ask Professor Madison.

"Mildred Cruz requested you," he says. "Their editor has an idea for you to work on. If you'd like to use it as your assignment for this course, you're free to do so."

"Okay. Maybe I will." I nod slowly as I walk away from him and head to my computer.

I'm grateful for the opportunity. Milly Cruz has always been like an aunt to me. She doesn't know about my summer fling with her son, so she has no reason to feel any type of way about me. I emailed her, letting her know that I received my assignment, and was told she had something in mind for me to work on. Then, I search some more about the drug scandal in my school and talk to a couple of my peers about it. Before I know it, it's time for me to go to work at the coffee shop. I pack up my things and check my email one last time before logging off. When I see one from Milly, I click it quickly and read through it.

Misty,

I'm so happy you'll be interning for us.

We have something in mind for you to work on. Your contact for this assignment will be Valerie, who works out of our Chapel Hill office. I looped her into this email so that you two can figure out when a good time to meet would be, and she can explain the assignment. I'm excited.

Big things ahead for you!

Xo,

Milly

Chapter Two

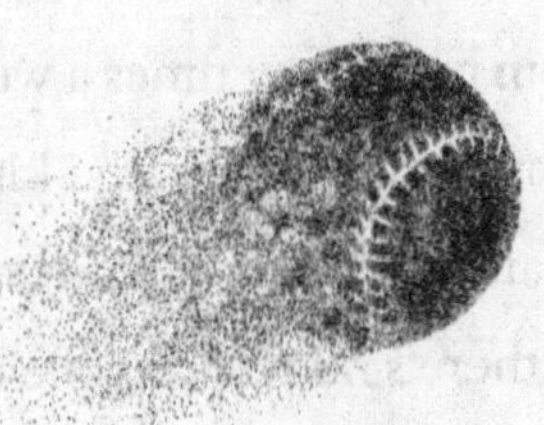

I'M STILL SMILING WHEN I STEP INTO THE COFFEE SHOP. MY coworker, Archer, is mid-conversation when he spots me and raises an eyebrow.

"Don't quit on me now, Misty."

I laugh. "Why would you think I'm here to quit?"

"Because you're smiling. That means you either got enough money for your fancy little shoes, or you got the internship you've been waiting for."

"If you must know, I did get the internship." I smile wider as I walk behind the counter and clock in on the computer screen. I glance over at him as I finish up. "But I'm not quitting."

"Good." He places a hand over his chest and breathes out a relieved breath. "I don't know what I'd do without my employee who's always late but also always willing to pick up extra shifts."

I shake my head and roll my eyes but keep smiling. Archer Roth has quickly become one of my favorite people with his dry humor and infectious smile. His family moved here two years ago from New York, and his parents rapidly opened up a slew of businesses, including *Night Owl Coffee*. Mr. and Mrs. Roth are in here a few times a week, but they've let Archer take the reins in many ways, so I kind of view him as my boss. My boss and friend. Soleil doesn't understand that concept. She says there's no way anyone can remain just friends with someone as good-looking as Archer.

Soleil likes to hang out here all day sometimes, using the excuse that she's doing homework, but I know she's just trying to get Archer's attention. I'm pretty sure he knows it too. I just don't understand why he's not making any moves. He's definitely good-looking if you like fair-skinned, tall, skinny guys with light brown eyes that match their hair and an easy smile. The quintessential boy next door, if you will. From an outside perspective, one look at Soleil, with her mile-long legs and a sex appeal that oozes out of her, would have you thinking she's nowhere near his playing field. Still, once you get to know her, you realize that underneath the bombshell is a colossal nerd that's compatible with Archer. I think he only sees the bombshell, though, and is blinded to how much she's attracted to him.

"So, what's up with the internship? Who'd you get? ESPN?"

"Cruz Media." I shoot him a look. "Two people got ESPN, though, so they were participating this year."

"Damn those people."

"Yes, damn those people." I laugh. "It's fine though; Cruz Media personally requested me, and they're pretty amazing."

"Personally requested?" Archer raises an eyebrow. "Is this your ex-boyfriend's family's company?"

"Yes."

"Do you think he requested you?"

"No." I frown. "Of course not. They're family friends. We go way back. They don't even know he was ever a boyfriend."

"Hm."

"Hm, what?" I place a hand on my hip. "I'm telling you, he had nothing to do with it."

"What's your assignment?" He brushes past me when the door opens, and a new customer walks in.

"I don't have one yet. I'm waiting for the person in charge of the Chapel Hill offices to contact me."

"Either way, I'm sure it'll be exciting," Archer says, pausing to smile at Ms. Roberta, who's a regular here. "Espresso with a shot of oat milk?"

"You know it." Ms. Roberta winks and looks over at me

as she taps the cardholder to pay. "I haven't seen you in here on a Monday in a while."

"I was only working weekends." I move to fill up the cup in the espresso machine and push it in, clicking the button. I wink at Ms. Roberta, who's already moving to the other side of the counter. "I'll be here all week now, though."

"Oh, what happened? Did Austin quit?"

"Yeah right. Like Austin would quit as long as Misty's working here," Archer says with a chuckle.

"He's still pining over you? Girl, give him a chance!"

"He's not pining over me," I say, unable to keep the smile from my face even though this conversation is ridiculous.

"He's absolutely pining over you." Archer shoots me a look.

"Whatever. The point is, Austin still works here and I will be here all week," I say, emphasizing that last bit.

"Most of the week," Archer says. "You don't work Friday."

"True. There's a rager on Friday that I don't want to miss," I say to Ms. Roberta, who blinks at me, shaking her head.

"You do you, honey. You're only young once."

I grin as I tap the milk container on the counter, waiting for it to set, and start pouring it in slowly, in the shape of a leaf. It's something I mastered from Archer, who can create almost anything. We have a few little stencils we can use to draw with cinnamon powder, but using milk is definitely a favorite of mine. It's greatly satisfying to see the shapes come to life, even knowing they'll disappear the moment the customer takes a few sips. The smile on their faces, though, is priceless. Ms. Roberta rewards me with a big smile as she takes the mug and thanks me, walking away to her usual table in the corner.

"I'm surprised Soleil isn't here," Archer says.

"I'm surprised you notice considering that when she is here you completely ignore her." I raise an eyebrow. "Are you ever going to ask her out?"

"I'll ask her out when you go out with Austin." He raises an eyebrow back at me.

"This is a completely different situation. Soleil is into you and you're into her. Austin is just a friend."

"You've said a million times how cute he is."

"Because he is cute! It doesn't mean I want to date him."

"Right, since you don't date anyone."

"That's not true." I frown. "I date all the time."

"You went out with that Dylan guy three times before you lost interest."

"Actually, I lost interest after date number one, but I was being nice."

"You are not nice." Archer chuckles. "You're not nice at all. You went out with him a second and third time because he was going to parties you hadn't been invited to."

"Yeah, well." I shrug a shoulder, not bothering to hide a smile.

He's not wrong about that and he's not wrong about the dating thing. My first boyfriend broke my heart and told me what we'd had was just a summer fling, which was awful for me since my feelings for him went deep. I'd completely fallen in love with him during those summer months and he just . . . shrugged me off like I was nothing. I had a boyfriend freshman year and we broke it off after six months when we both decided to focus on school. Of course, when anyone tells you they're going to focus on school what they really mean is they don't really want to be tied down to you anymore. After him, I dated someone else for a few months until I found out he was still seeing other people behind my back. That was when I decided to forget dating in college. I figure if I find someone and it works out, great, but I'm not going to put myself out there just to be disappointed again. As for Austin, he's asked me out twice and I gently turned him down both times. He's cute, he's funny, but he's too nice and Archer isn't wrong when he says I'm not, so I'd rather not hurt the guy's feelings.

"If you ask out Austin, I'll ask out Soleil," Archer says.

I roll my eyes, but mull it over. Soleil has been waiting for this for a year now. It's not like she's crying herself to sleep over it or anything, but I know her and I know she's dying to date this guy for reasons I will never understand.

"You better not chicken out," I say after a moment.

"I won't." He swallows and I can tell he's already trying to figure out how or when he's going to ask her out. I shoot him a look that hopefully conveys I'm serious about him not chickening out and he says, "I'm not going to chicken out."

"Fine." I take my phone out of the pocket of my apron and text Austin asking him if he wants to grab dinner on Friday night. Not even a second later, he texts back the word *absolutely*. I show him the screen.

"No way." Archer laughs. "Was he waiting for you to text? How'd he even answer that fast?"

"You have until the end of the day to ask her out."

"I don't even know if she's—" Archer's words die down when the door opens and Soleil walks in. His ears turn red as he looks over at me. "I guess it's showtime."

I flash him a thumbs-up and go back to cleaning up the counter so that I can start preparing Soleil's chai latte. As I do, I glance over a few times and watch as they talk. From the look on her face I know he finally did ask her out and from his red cheeks, I know he's still embarrassed. Once I serve her drink and slide the mug over to the front of the counter, I take my phone out and check my email quickly, seeing one from Valerie. I open and read through it before shooting one back to confirm our meeting time. My pulse quickens as I put my phone away. I'm really doing this.

Chapter Three

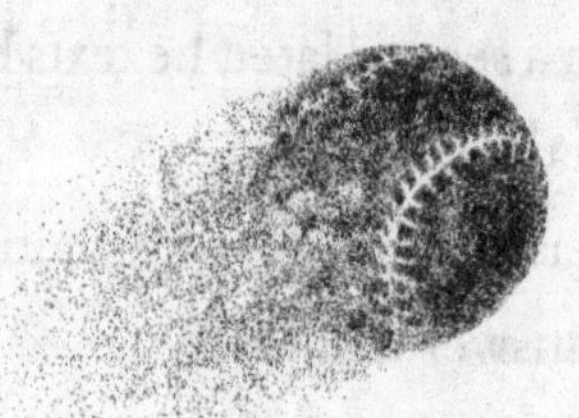

"**W**HAT WE HAD IN MIND WAS FOR THE PERSON following the team to stay in a house with them, but since you're a woman, and excuse me for even bringing that into the equation, we have legal issues to consider. We have to make sure you're okay living with three guys," Rodney, the Cruz Media legal counselor says.

"I'm not sure that I am," I say.

"The alternative would be for you to move next door and be at their place at six thirty a.m.," Valerie says quickly.

"I don't understand the legality factor," one of the baseball players, a blond with striking blue eyes, says. "Is it because you think we're a threat to her in any way?"

"That's always a concern when people share a coed

space." Rodney shoots him a look. "You have a party, people get drunk, things happen."

"You have to know that we would never do anything to hurt her." The blond's eyes widen looking between myself and Rodney.

"Not if you want to live," Mitch adds.

I feel myself go hot and cold at the same time and bite my lip. I hate that his words, as fake as they are, affect me. When I look over at him, he's leaning back in his chair, long legs sprawled out, looking at me with those seductive green eyes. I snap my attention away quickly, unwilling to allow him to get to me. *Not today, Mitch. Not today.*

"We're telling this story because a group of athletes decided to do something that no one expected them to do, so forgive me for not trusting what anyone's motives are," Valerie says.

The blond guys shakes his head. Mitchell sighs heavily, kicking his foot out even further as he fixes his dark wavy hair underneath the baseball cap before putting it back on. He leaves it backwards. The three of them are wearing their hats like that and I don't know what it is about backwards caps that makes me hot and bothered, but I swear it does it for me.

"Just move her in next door," Valerie says again. "If I was in her position, I'd definitely want my own space."

"I have my own space," I say. "I have an apartment."

"Thirty minutes away," she responds. "By signing up for this, you're agreeing to go to their meetings, practices, away games. It's a lot."

"It's a two-week gig," Mitchell adds, lowering his voice slightly. "You might as well stay close."

"Of course you'd say that." I roll my eyes and glance away quickly when he smirks.

Our brief dating history aside, he can be a real jerk sometimes. My dad is Mitch's godfather, and that always meant seeing him once or twice a year. For a while, my sister and I were able to escape those visits, but ever since we've been in the same place, he's unavoidable. It doesn't matter that I go to school on the other side of town since we go to different universities. It doesn't matter that I've made myself unavailable to him to the point that my resting bitch face deserves an Academy Award. Every time I see Mitchell, he comes on to me. Every single time. Whether it be innuendoes or straight up asking me out. It's as if he enjoys watching my discomfort, because even though to someone else I'd look like an ice queen, Mitchell knows me better than that and he knows I'm affected. I sigh heavily and look at Valerie, who's waiting for me to chime in about the living arrangement.

"When do I move in?"

"Tomorrow?" she asks rather than says. "There's a dinner party at your uncle's restaurant. I can give you the key there. The place is fully furnished, so you only need to bring your clothes."

"I have plans tomorrow night."

"Plans?" That's Mitchell. "What kind of plans are more important than writing this piece?"

"The kind I simply cannot break." I shoot him a look.

"So you wouldn't be able to make the dinner party?" Valerie asks.

"I guess I can try." I bite my lip as I think about my options. I can always take Austin as my date to said dinner party and kill two birds with one stone. I look at Valerie. "Can I bring a date?"

"Of course you can," Valerie says.

"Why would you bring a date?" Mitchell says at the exact same time.

"Mind your business, Mitchell." Valerie glances over at him. "This has nothing to do with you."

I smile while Mitchell glowers. Maybe this assignment won't be as difficult as I thought.

Chapter Four

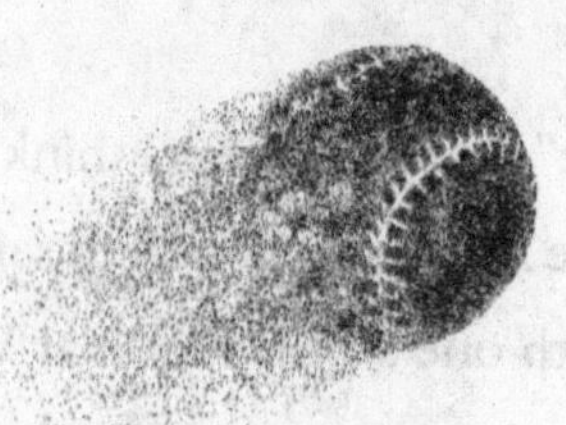

ARCHER SHAKES HIS HEAD AS I TELL HIM ABOUT MY ASSIGNMENT, and again when I tell him I'm taking Austin as my date to the dinner tonight.

"Are you trying to make your ex-boyfriend jealous?"

"What? No." I scoff. "Mitch isn't the jealous type. He's the type who thinks everyone is lucky to share the air he breathes."

Archer laughs. "I bet Austin wasn't thrilled to learn your first date was going to be surrounded by jocks."

"I gave him an out. He seemed to be totally okay with going."

"Or maybe he doesn't want to cancel on you because he doesn't think he'll get another shot." Archer raises an eyebrow.

"In any event, we're going tonight." I smile. "What's up with you and Soleil?"

"We're also going out tonight."

"Where are you taking her?"

"Yeah right." Archer chuckles. "You think I'm going to tell you and spoil the surprises I have planned?"

"Surprises. Multiple." I raise my eyebrows. "Someone is feeling very sure of himself and this date."

"Or I decided to pile up all the date ideas I've been saving in case she turns me down for a second."

I laugh. "That's actually not a bad idea."

"I'm sure you'll be hearing from one of us by the end of the night. I hope it's me showing off and not her complaining."

"It never occurred to me how weird it might be for two of my friends to start dating." I lean against the counter and watch as he finishes capping the new bottles of whipped cream.

"We're not dating." He smiles. "Yet."

"Yet." I smile back.

"So, at what time is Austin picking you up?"

"Six thirty. The dinner starts at seven. I figure I should be there a little early to get the key to my new place from Valerie."

"New place, huh? Where will you be living?"

"I have no idea, but I assume it'll be right by here, since I'll be covering the UNC baseball team and all."

"I guess this means you won't be complaining about the track to get here anymore." He shoots me a look. "Or get here late."

"I guess so," I say in a sing-song voice, rolling my eyes. "I was late once."

"One too many times."

"And I called your mom about it."

"And my mom is rarely ever here so that was mistake number one."

I sigh. "Okay, Arch. I get it."

"Good." He smiles. "What do you think I should wear tonight?"

I laugh. "I would help you, but my boss is a bit of a jerk and wants me to only work the entire time I'm here."

"Oh, come on, Misty," he calls out as I walk away from him with things in my hand to go wash.

"Sorry. Maybe another time when I'm not working," I call out and laugh as the door opens with a new customer.

Once I'm in the back, I text Soleil to let her know what's going on. I haven't been able to really talk to her since our schedules aren't coinciding the way they usually do. She texts back a few minutes later with a simple: *OMG. Don't fall for that asshole again!* I text back assuring that I won't, then frown to myself. Did I really paint Mitchell as an asshole? I mean, not that he doesn't deserve it for breaking my heart, but the memories I have of us together were definitely good ones. I push those aside and focus on the only one that matters, when he told me he couldn't possibly love me, and stick to that one. It still hurts just as much as it did when I was seventeen. I'm not sure that kind of pain just goes away. Maybe this will be for the best. It'll bring closure to what I never had.

Chapter Five

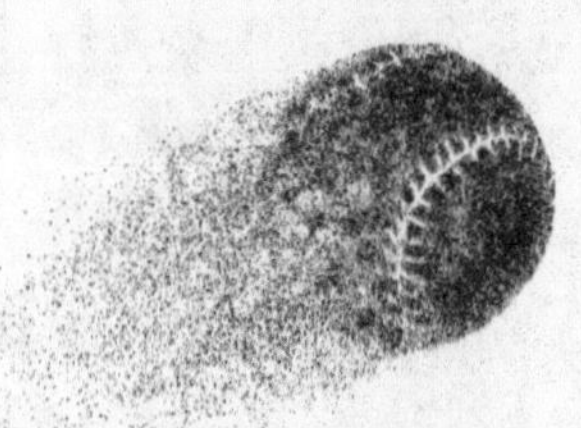

"WHEW. I'M GLAD I DRESSED UP FOR THIS." AUSTIN EYES me up and down, checking me out before meeting my gaze again. "You look amazing."

"Thank you." I smile. "So do you."

He's wearing black slacks and a white button-down. He's wearing the uniform the waiters at my uncle's restaurant wear, but I don't want to tell him that because he went the extra mile and I was the one who made him dress up for this date. Besides, he looks handsome. Austin has that boy-next-door charm. He's sweet, with a kind smile and a great personality. The fact that I don't like him in that way is a reflection of how messed up I am and not the other way around.

"Shall we?" He offers me his arm as if we're going to prom in the fifties.

On our way to the restaurant, we small talk about school and what our plans are once we graduate. Austin has two more semesters to go, while I'll be finished after this one. He's telling me all about his parents' flooring company, which he plans to work at once he's done with his business degree, when we pull into the parking lot.

"This is your uncle's place, right?" He turns the car off and looks over at me as we get out of the car.

"Yep."

"I'm guessing your sister is long gone by now. I can't believe she's engaged to an NFL player." He chuckles. "But I guess y'all are used to famous people, with your dad being their doctor and all."

"I wouldn't say we're used to famous people. I guess we know a lot of athletes though, yeah." I smile. "And some are famous."

"That's wild."

"I guess." I let out a laugh as we walk inside the restaurant.

It's something our friends have always been impressed with, but doesn't really get to me, probably because most of the famous athletes we know are people we grew up with and my brother-in-law is one of them. As are Mitchell and Maverick, if either of them end up going pro. We walk through the arch of baby blue balloons in the front of the restaurant and stop walking, not knowing where to go next.

There are probably twenty large tables set up, with people filling each of them.

"If I didn't know any better, I'd think this was a baby shower," Austin whispers beside me, making me laugh.

It's letting out that laugh that makes me realize how wound up I've been. It's not like I'm intimidated by anyone here or this date with Austin. Yet, the heaviness in my chest doesn't seem to go away. Anxiety was what my doctor diagnosed me with. My parents made me go and see someone. As if I needed a professional to tell me what I already knew. I don't know when exactly I developed it. As a teenager, I'd always been outgoing and fun, and then something changed. I began to worry more. About everything. My mother pinned it back to when I was a worry-wart of a child before she began to question if something traumatic happened to me in New York when I was gone for a year. That wasn't the case though. In any event, I'd been given medicine to help and developed an intolerance to them before being introduced to medicinal marijuana. I'm trying not to rely on it all the time unless I need it, not because I feel I'm getting addicted or anything, but because I hate relying on anything, or anyone.

"So, I think that's a seating chart." Austin points at poster board a few steps from where we are and we walk over there. Sure enough, it's a seating chart. I find my name with a plus one beside it and tell Austin, who smiles. "Plus one, huh?

Is that because you weren't sure who you were bringing as your date?"

"If we didn't have a date planned, I wouldn't have brought anyone at all."

"In that case, I don't mind being a plus one." Austin smiles.

We head over to table nine, where I see Valerie sitting with a man dressed in a black suit. When we reach the table, she smiles up at me and introduces me to her husband, Rick. I introduce them to Austin as we sit down beside them, quickly making small talk. While Rick and Austin are talking about Austin's side hustle of collecting and selling Pokémon cards, Valerie goes into her purse and hands me a single key on a key ring.

"I'll email you the information right now, so you have it," she says. "The address and all that fun stuff." She smiles. "I think it'll be fun, I mean, who doesn't want to be in close quarters with some fun baseball players?"

"Right." I can't imagine why that would be fun, but I give a little laugh as I put away the key in my own purse and Valerie begins typing out the email with specifics right beside me.

As I'm reading over what she just sent, I see people approach our table from the corner of my eye. When I look up, I see Mitchell, Rodney, and Dylan sit down across from us. I met Rodney the other day at the Cruz Media office. Dylan looks between myself and Austin a couple of times before shaking his head as if he can't believe I'd bring a date here. As if he has any right to think that at all, being that we only went on a handful of dates and didn't hook up. Not all the way hooked up anyway. Mitchell is stone faced and looks upset and I don't even bother to try to decipher that emotion coming from him. It seems that more often than not, he's upset when he's around me these days. It doesn't really make a difference to me. Rodney introduces himself to Austin and Valerie's husband and the other two follow suit.

"I just gave Misty the key to her new apartment," Valerie says.

"You're moving?" Austin asks.

"Only temporarily." I smile.

"But you're still going to work, right?"

"I'm actually moving closer to the coffee shop, so yeah."

"You may want to reconsider the coffee shop gig," Mitchell says. When I look up at him, he winks. "I'm going to keep you pretty busy the next two weeks."

Even as I narrow my eyes on him, I feel my face go hot.

"So you think she should give up her paying job to focus only on one that doesn't pay her at all?" Austin asks, jumping in before I can.

"I think the internship will provide a lot of good paying opportunities for her, so yes," Mitchell responds.

"If you think something that's going to pay her in a year

or two will be enough to satisfy her, then you don't know Misty at all." Austin shrugs a shoulder. "Besides, she's capable of doing both jobs and doing them well."

I've never been into the knight-in-shining-armor thing, but in this moment, I could kiss Austin for this. So I do. I smile as I look over at him, lean in, and kiss him on the lips. It's a chaste kiss, but I hope he feels the gratitude in it.

"You should've brought me to this a month ago." He chuckles when I pull away. I'm still smiling when I glance over at Mitchell and Dylan, who are both scowling, and I realize that I truly don't care what either of them have to say about my life. Austin is right, they don't know me. Mitchell may have been able to use that line and even his knowledge years ago, but not anymore. The Misty I am now is very different from the Misty I was when I was seventeen and it's that thought that gives me the confidence I need to know that my new living arrangement will be perfectly okay.

Chapter Six

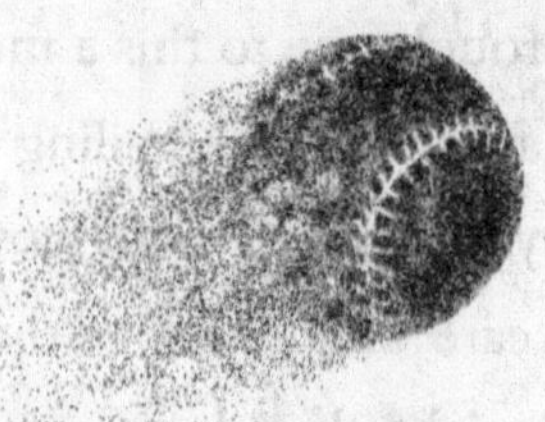

MY EYES POP OPEN, BUT MY ALARM HASN'T EVEN GONE OFF. I look over at the time and see it's five thirty. What the hell woke me up? A sound. A ringing sound. I look at my clock once again, then at my phone. It wasn't either of my alarms. Then, the doorbell rings. I sigh, letting my head hit my pillow again before I force myself to get out of bed. The apartment isn't huge, it's a one bedroom, though, which means I have to walk out of the room, past the living room slash dining room and kitchen on my way to the door. It's weird waking up in a new, fully furnished place, that I had nothing to do with decorating, but I like it. It's cute and chic. I rub my eyes before looking through the peephole and find Mitchell standing on the other side. I pull the door open.

"What are you doing here? Did something happen?"

"It's five thirty." He raises an eyebrow as he takes me in fully, his gaze slowly falling on every inch of me. It might affect me if I wasn't so tired.

"I set my alarm for six thirty. That's what Valerie said."

"Clearly, Valerie doesn't know about my morning run."

"Why exactly do I have to know about your morning run this early in the morning?" I blink and start closing the door. "Come back when you're done with that."

"Come with me." He places the tip of his sneaker on the bottom of the door, so I can't continue closing it.

"On your run?" I nearly shout, then lower my voice to a whisper when I remember normal people are sleeping at this time. "Are you insane?"

"You're supposed to be writing an article on college athletes, aren't you?"

"Yeah."

"So why not experience a day in the life the unfiltered way?"

I take a step back, lips pursing as I consider this invitation. He has a point. I do want to do the best job I can and this would ensure that it happens. Besides, when else would I get a completely unfiltered view of the ins and outs of this? It's not like I ever cared to before. My sister played volleyball for UNC and besides going to some games here and there, I didn't show much interest in behind the scenes. I mean, it wasn't until she got kicked off the team that I realized someone could even be kicked off the team for something other than poor grades or cheating. I turn my eyes to Mitchell again, who's still staring at me, waiting, and nod once.

"Give me five minutes."

He fights a smile as he nods back and steps into my apartment. I disappear into my bedroom, shutting the door behind me, as I rummage through my things in search for workout clothes that I can wear beyond athleisure. My family is pretty athletic. Dad used to play baseball, Mom has always worked out, my sister played volleyball most of her life. I grew up in dance, and once the fun of it was over for me and I quit, I kind of fell off the bandwagon before Mom put an end to my indulgences and made me start going to Pilates with her. I used to go running with my sister sometimes when she was still living here, but I never really liked it. Some people say they find mental clarity while they run. The only thing I found was sore muscles and exhaustion followed by overeating because I was so damn hungry after the run. In any event, as I brush my teeth and pull my long dark hair into a high ponytail, I mentally prepare myself for my run with Mitch. I may not be the athlete of the family, but my competitive nature still runs deep.

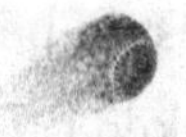

We're not even half a mile in when I stop running, put my hands on my knees, and focus on breathing.

"Come on, Misty. You've got to be kidding. You're in shape."

I don't even look up as I stick my middle finger out to him. Fuck him and his freakishly athletic figure. When we were seventeen and I dated him, he had perfectly etched muscles, but this Mitchell is beyond perfectly etched. He has muscles on muscles on muscles. He's not body-builder big or anything. He has the kind of frame where if he's fully clothed, you know he works out, but that's all you'd assume. It was the only thing I'd assumed until he took his shirt off a minute ago and swung it over his muscled shoulder. He's walking back over to where I am when I stand upright. I feel like I'm dying and he looks like he's on a fucking stroll.

"I'm tired." I take a deep breath. "I don't normally work out at five in the freaking morning."

"This is my daily run, not my workout. I don't lift till nine."

I balk. "What?"

"Let's just finish the mile and we can walk back," he says.

"Fine." I take another deep breath and start jogging beside him.

At least he's slowed his pace from Usain Bolt to regular person and I'm feeling pretty good about the rest of this jog, especially since it'll never happen again. Today I am definitely going to go along with the following him everywhere thing, especially since I don't have to go to school or work, but tomorrow I'll only be able to do some of the things. When we reach the end of the trail, he stops running and I do the same. He gives me a second to catch my breath before turning around and walking in the direction we just came from.

"So, you run this trail every day?" I ask.

"Every morning, except Sundays."

"How many times do you run it?"

"Four."

"Four?" I blink up at him. "It would take me a year to work up to that."

"You stay in shape." He eyes my bare stomach. "I've seen you jogging with Jo."

"First of all, I went jogging with Jo like four times and you happened to see me one of those times. Second, Jo only runs one mile a day. Third, I do Pilates. It's much more . . . effective for this." I signal toward my displayed abs. "Which, at the risk of sounding like a total douche, is really all I care about."

"That's fair." Mitch lets out a deep chuckle that I feel all the way to my core. "So, how'd it go with your date?"

"It went well."

"Not well enough for him to stay over though."

"Do you judge how every date does by whether or not they stay over?"

"Yes."

I shake my head. "That's why you're still single."

"Why are *you* still single?" He shoots me a look.

"I don't know. I guess I like it this way. There's a certain freedom that comes from not being tied down to a man."

"There's a certain freedom that comes with being tied down by a man." His eyes smolder as he says the words and I can't not think about him tying me down to a surface.

"Yeah." I look away quickly. "Well, maybe I'll experiment with that with Austin."

"Shame. Here I was hoping you'd experiment with me."

"Mitch." I stop walking just outside of the apartment building and turn to him. "This is an assignment for me. Nothing more. I can't have you throwing things like that at me right now."

"Because I still affect you."

"Yes." I keep my eyes on his. "Even though you shouldn't."

"Maybe if you gave me a chance, we could both get over this once and for all."

"Really?" I let out a laugh, shaking my head as I move to brush past him and walk into the building. "No, thank you, Mitchell."

"I'm just saying, it might not be such a bad idea."

"It's a terrible idea." I shoot him a look that begs for him to drop it.

He does and pushes the elevator button and we take it up to the tenth floor, where we both get off and head toward our respective apartments. As he stops in front of his and I walk by, I hear loud voices inside and remember he lives with two other guys on the team. Mitch doesn't move to go inside. He merely stands outside, holding his key, waiting for me to go into mine.

"Maybe we can do this again tomorrow."

"You want to add torture to the list of requirements for this assignment?" I raise an eyebrow.

"Aw, come on. You enjoyed it." His lip turns up slightly.

"It wasn't terrible." I purse my lips as I turn the key to my apartment and open the door. "I'll see you in a bit."

"See you in a bit." He gives a nod, looking like he wants to add more to that statement, but I disappear into my apartment before he gets a chance.

It's not until I'm in my kitchen, which is also fully stocked, that I realize my heart is beating out of control and it has nothing to do with the run and everything to do with Mitchell. I shake my head at myself. I cannot go down that road again. And I won't. I've been able to resist the temptation that is Mitchell Cruz for years now and this will be no different.

Chapter Seven

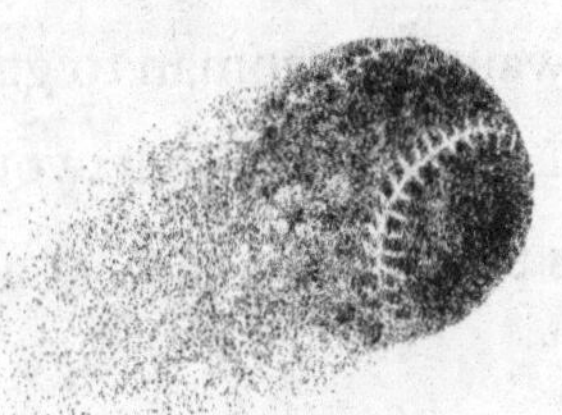

"YOU'RE LATE," DYLAN SAYS AS HE OPENS THE DOOR FOR me.

"Good morning to you too." I step inside and wait for him to close the door. Normally, I would just let his poor attitude slide, but since this job depends on me somewhat getting along with them, at least enough for them to open up to me, I figure I should address this now. He leans against the door and crosses his arms, waiting. "I just want to make sure we're cool, you know, since we're going to have to spend time together for this."

"We're cool. Why wouldn't we be cool? Because you ghosted me?" He pushes off the door. "I'm just glad Mitchell was willing to let it go."

"Mitchell?" I feel myself frown. "What does he have to do with any of this?"

"That night I met you he told me to stay away from you and I didn't take his advice. I didn't realize he was saying it because you'd already broken his heart, otherwise, I would have stayed away from you." He shoots me a look. "To be clear, you didn't break my heart, but he's my brother and I never wanted a woman to get between us. We're good though. I'm not going to let you ghosting me get in the way of this project. We have a reputation to fix and that'll be on you."

"I . . . okay. Sure." I blink, trying to process all of this, but my mind seems to be stuck on the fact that Mitchell says I broke his heart.

It's laughable. Stupid. Did he have a completely different memory of how things went down? Did he live in some sort of alternate universe where he told me he couldn't be in love with me and his heart was the one that broke? Dylan walks past me and I take one more second to push the thoughts away before following him fully into the apartment. It's bigger than mine, which makes sense since this is a three bedroom. The living room is huge, the kitchen is a decent size, and there's a staircase that winds up to a second floor. Surprisingly, it's neat and smells clean. Rodney walks out of one of the three doors near the living room and smiles at me.

"Hey, Misty."

"Hey." I smile back, then go back to looking around. "Do you guys even live here? It's so clean."

Rodney chuckles. "Well, you know Mitch, so I'm sure you know how anal he is about things."

"Mitch is anal about anal," Dylan adds with a snicker.

"I heard that, you bastard," Mitch calls out from upstairs, making the guys laugh.

I tilt my head back, but I can't see him from this angle. He starts coming down the stairs before I get a chance to move and I get a glimpse of a shirtless Mitch, pulling his shirt over his head and sinking his fingers into his hair as he tries to somewhat fix it. The fact that my heart leaps a little from that small display does not bode well with my plan of not letting him affect me while I do this project. He glances at me, gives me a full once-over, and meets my eyes.

"Why are you not wearing workout clothes?"

"Because I showered after someone forced me to run a mile and it didn't feel like an athleisure kind of day." I look at the three of them. They are definitely dressed to work out. I remember that in my half-asleep state, Mitchell mentioned a lifting session that was happening later and it dawns on me that when he said his run was a warm-up he did alone it was because it wasn't required. "I'm not going to lift weights with you," I say finally.

"You're just tagging along for moral support?" Mitch raises an eyebrow. "I thought you were here to walk a mile in our shoes."

"I just ran a mile in your shoes." I set a hand on my hip.

"You walked half of it." He smirks.

"I'm not the one on a sports scholarship."

"Ohh, she got you there," one of the guys says, while the other laughs.

Mitch doesn't even crack a smile as his serious green eyes stay on mine and for some crazy, irrational reason it makes me want to do as he's telling me to do, because once again, he's not wrong. I did sign up to walk a mile in their shoes. My head battles with my heart for a moment. I'm nothing if not rebellious. I hate being told what to do. *But you want to do great in this assignment.* Finally, I sigh.

"I guess it wouldn't kill me to do some squats."

"You have three minutes." Mitch looks at his watch. "We have to leave."

"I'll take two." I'm running out of their apartment as I say it.

I change quickly into leggings, a sports bra, and a thin hoodie, grabbing my sneakers as I head back to the door. I open it as I'm putting on my lace-free sneakers and find Mitchell standing on the other side.

"Holy crap." I take a step back. "You scared me."

"I was just coming to let you know the guys are on their way down. We needed to leave like two minutes ago."

"Well, I'm ready. I could've met you there." I shoot him a look as we walk to the elevator.

"Then you wouldn't be walking a mile in my shoes, would you?"

"You're taking this more seriously than I am."

"I've noticed." He glances over at me as the elevator door closes and it starts descending. "I wouldn't be proud of that if I were you."

I roll my eyes. "You sound like my father."

"Well, I respect your father, so forgive me if that comment isn't exactly cutting."

"When did you become such a bore anyway?" I cross my arms.

"A bore?" He chuckles. "I am not a bore. I just know how to separate my work life from my party life."

"Work life?" I let out a laugh. "You're in college. You play baseball. You don't have a job."

"I can't work right now." He waits for me to step out of the elevator when we reach the lobby.

"Hm." My stomach growls. I set a hand over it.

"You didn't have breakfast?"

"You did?" My eyes widen. "When? How?"

"I had a protein shake when I got back from my half-assed mile run."

"Well, I had coffee. And a banana. Obviously not enough," I say as my stomach growls even louder. "Why is it so quiet in here?"

Mitchell chuckles, shaking his head as we walk out to the front, but doesn't comment on my hunger as we pile into his two-door BMW and head to the school. The guys are talking about practice and a teammate who's been out with an injury and may be coming back and I'm trying to absorb everything, but my growling stomach keeps me from truly paying attention so I focus on the buildings we're driving by. Without a word, Mitchell makes a right and parks in front of a popular smoothie chain, gets out of the car, leaving the three of us confused, before he walks back out with a huge cup in his hand.

"You didn't even ask us if we wanted anything," one of them says behind me.

"I could've totally killed a Hulk right now," Dylan adds.

Mitchell says nothing. He hands me the large cup, which I take, as he puts his seat belt on and backs out of the parking space.

"Are you going to drink it or not?" He shoots me a look as he stops the car by the exit of the shopping center.

"It's . . . you got this for me?" I feel myself frown.

"I don't hear anyone else's stomach growling."

"Mine is growling," Dylan says. "You never buy me smoothies."

Mitch ignores this. He continues to look at me as I look anywhere but his eyes and rip the paper from the straw and plug it into the lid.

"Thank you." I look at him again. "I need your number so I can send you money."

"Don't insult me." He looks away from me and keeps driving.

I take a long sip of the smoothie and close my eyes with a sigh. "I really needed this."

"Yeah, tomorrow, after the mile, eat something."

"Tomorrow?" My eyes pop open. I glance over at him. "I work at seven."

"We run at five then." He shrugs a shoulder like it's no big deal to wake up at four thirty in the freaking morning to do something I absolutely detest.

"As a rule, I don't do things I don't enjoy."

"As a rule." He chuckles.

"That's a good rule," Dylan says from the back seat. Mitchell shoots him a look in the rearview, to which Dylan responds, "What? It's a good rule."

"How'd it not work out between the two of you?" Rodney asks. "That's literally Dylan's life motto."

"YOLO," Dylan says.

"That's Drake's motto," Mitch responds.

"And mine."

"And mine," I say, taking another sip of the smoothie.

"Which is why I'm wondering why things didn't work out," Rodney says again. I feel my face grow hot, but I don't make a show out of it. Thankfully, I'm in the front seat and can just look out the window and let Dylan answer this.

"Misty says she'd never date an athlete," Dylan says. "I respect that."

"Is that true?" Mitch glances over at me as he parks the car in front of Boshamer Stadium.

I get out of the car quickly, pulling the lever so my seat moves forward and the guys can get out. While they get their bags out of the trunk, I scroll through my emails and texts and sip on the smoothie, then follow behind them as they walk toward the building. Mitch slows down and walks beside me as I continue reading through the group text between myself, Soleil, and Jo.

"You never answered me," Mitch says, pulling my attention away from my phone and up at him, confused. "You really wouldn't date an athlete?"

"Oh." I let out a laugh. "Been there, done that."

"Right, but that was a long time ago." His brows pull in.

"It was and it wasn't." I shrug.

"So if I ask you out on a date, you'd say no."

My heart leaps, slamming into its cage. I swallow. "I'd definitely say no."

"Hm."

He makes no further comment as we walk inside the building, but if I know one thing about Mitchell it's that he can't leave anything alone.

Chapter Eight

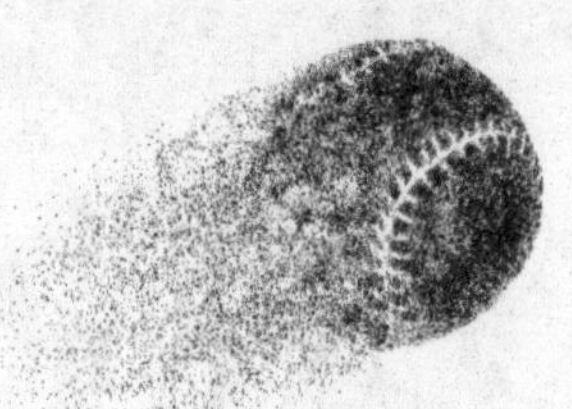

THE COFFEE SHOP IS BUZZING WHEN I WALK INSIDE. THERE are people everywhere, sitting, standing, talking, working. There's something to be said about what spring does to people. Both Archer and Austin are behind the bar making drinks and taking orders. I speed up and walk back there, going into the back room to put my things down before pulling an apron over my head and tying it around my waist as I say hi to the guys and clock in. Austin and I haven't spoken since our date a couple of nights ago and there's no time right now while it's this busy in here. I continue taking orders while they make the drinks and once the door stops opening and new customers stop coming in, the three of us let out a collective breath and lean against the counter.

"So," Austin starts, "how's it going with the story?"

"It's going. I just had them drop me off here in between their lifting session and practice. I'll tell you what, I did not expect this to be the life of a college athlete. They just don't stop."

"And they don't even get paid," Archer says. "Are you including that in your article?"

"Of course. I mean, it is a valid point, right? The school can't make me ineligible for graduation for pointing out the obvious." I bite my lower lip, brows pinching. "Right?"

"They're literally facing charges right now," Austin says. "Those athletes, I mean. Who knows what will happen to the athletic departments."

"Yeah, didn't they want you guys to paint them in a good light?" Archer asks.

"Well, of course they do, but this is journalism. I'm not going to sugarcoat what's happening. Besides, the school not paying athletes is on the organizations, not on the athletes themselves."

"What do they say about it?" Austin pushes off the counter and faces me.

"I haven't asked."

"Let me know what they say when you do. I'm curious about that," Archer says as he also pushes off the counter and pushes the door that leads to the back. "I'll be right back."

"So," Austin says after a moment. "I know you've been busy, so I wasn't sure if I should call or text but text felt too impersonal since it's what we do now, not that I don't like what we do now, but I wasn't sure where you stood on maybe going out with me again." His face turns a deeper shade of red with each word he says before he finally shuts his mouth and glances away momentarily.

"I wouldn't . . ." I pause with a sigh. Now it's my turn to glance away as I gather my thoughts, finally settling on, "You know how much I like you."

"As a friend," he provides.

"Yes." I bite my lip, hoping my expression shows how regretful I am about it. "As a friend."

"I figured."

"I'm sorry." I shut my eyes. "I know it's super cliché, but it really isn't you, it's me."

"I know." The certainty in his tone makes my eyes pop open. "I know you're weird about dating, which is why I was surprised when you agreed to go out with me. I do wish things were different though."

"Me too." I try for a smile, but it feels weak.

"So, forget another date. I don't want things to be weird with us here or anything," he says. "How 'bout you drive me to Target after we close?"

"More Pokémon cards?" I let out a laugh.

"Hey, my connection there says the guy is restocking tonight."

"Sure." I shrug a shoulder. "It's not like I have anything going on."

To say the Target parking lot is crowded would be an understatement. Austin shifts in the passenger seat, swearing under his breath. I bite the inside of my cheek and look out the window to keep from laughing. This is not a guy who upsets easily, so this must be a big deal.

"He must have told other people." He starts typing furiously on his phone again. "By the time we get inside everything is going to be gone."

"Shouldn't we just go inside and see for ourselves?"

"Sure." He's out of the car before I can say another word.

I turn it off, grab my purse from the back seat, and rush after him. Inside the store, it looks like it does any other day, but there's a large crowd around the aisle beside the register.

"Wow," is all I can say. "I feel like I've entered an alternate universe. All of these people are here for Pokémon cards?"

"Yep." Austin exhales heavily. "Wait here."

I nod and step aside. There's no way I'm getting involved in a scuffle over trading cards. My phone buzzes in my back pocket and I'm grateful for the distraction. I take it out and look at the screen to find a text from an unknown, New York, number.

Hey. It's Mitch. Are you coming home any time soon?

My heart skips. *How'd you get my number?*

I never deleted it.

Why? It's not like you ever used it.

Did you want me to use it?

I start typing out a response, and then stop and delete it. I hate myself for being so emotionally invested in a man who broke my heart without a second thought, and that's the thing, I am emotionally invested. I'm not delusional enough to say that I'm not. It just kills me that I can't be emotionally invested in a guy like Austin instead. Or Dylan. Or anyone else I've even remotely tried to date through the years. After Mitch, there was one guy I dated for a little while and all I did was break his heart because he couldn't repair mine. It's taken years of rehearsing the cold-hearted bitch act. Years of acting like he doesn't affect me when he talks to me, flirts with me, tries to make moves on me. I've gotten to a point in my life where I stand on my own and know my worth. The next time

I fall, it won't be so hard because I never want to be in a place where I can't lift myself back up.

I put my phone away. It buzzes again in my pocket, but this time, I ignore it and look at the crowd of people buzzing around the trading cards. I never understood why people collect things, but these people seem to have formed a community around their interests and I definitely see the appeal in that.

Chapter Nine

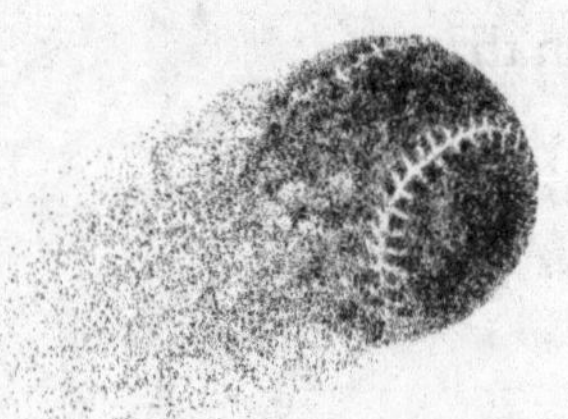

Mitch

KEEP STARING AT MY PHONE, THINKING MAYBE I'LL FIND A response from Misty, but nope. She ghosted me. The fact that she'd erased my number doesn't surprise me, but I have to admit it does sting a little. I know I messed things up with her. I just wish she'd move past it and give me another chance. As I remember what Dylan said about her not dating athletes, I set my phone down with a sigh. There's no denying that it's because of our history, but maybe she's willing to try again. I pick up my phone and text her again.

We're having a get together on the rooftop. You should go up there when you get here.

I hit send and sit back in my bean bag chair for two seconds before getting up and getting my ass in gear. We weren't having a get together at all, but we are now. I walk over to Dylan's room and knock on his door.

"We're having a get together tonight," I shout, knowing he probably has earbuds in. "Invite some people."

"Tell Rodney to get his DJ equipment out," Dylan calls out.

I walk toward Rodney's room, across from the living room, and knock on his door. Before I have a chance to say anything, he opens the door.

"Party?"

"Get together," I say.

"With DJ equipment?" He raises an eyebrow.

"Talk to your boy about that." I shrug. "Besides, you know the girls like it when you DJ."

"That's because you get to show off your dance skills. Swinging your hips and doing all your Rico Suave moves." He rolls his eyes.

"Hey, it's not my fault I have that Caribbean flavor."

"Right." He chuckles and walks toward the kitchen. "Do we even have any alcohol?"

"We should have a beer or two," I say. "I'll go grab some stuff after I change."

"It's a good thing Coach canceled practice tomorrow."

Rodney opens the fridge. "Yeah, we have two left. Definitely not enough for a rager."

"This is not a rager. It's a get together," I say again, though we both know every single one of our get togethers start out small and get bigger by the second. "On second thought, I'm going to grab the beers and vodka before I change."

"Just go down the street. They have beer and that fruity seltzer water people like."

"Yeah." I grab my keys and head out.

On my way to the store, I check my phone again. Still nothing from Misty. I shake it off and call my brother instead.

"Yo," Maverick says upon answering.

"Yo. We're having a get together tonight if you want to stop by."

"Another one?" He yawns. "I just got home from the gym. I'm beat, bro. I'm waiting for Rocky to get home. It's her turn to make dinner."

I laugh. "Is it ever your turn to make dinner?"

"I made dinner last night."

"You made it or Mom sent you Uber Eats?"

"Fuck you." He chuckles.

"Just come over with Rocky. They canceled practice for us tomorrow."

He pauses. "Damn. Does it have something to do with the investigation?"

"They didn't say. Have you heard anything?"

"Nope. My guys are clean."

"None of the hockey players were involved?" I frown.

"Nope. Only baseball, football, and some basketball, but not many. Mostly football."

"Shit." I exhale. "Have you spoken to Jag?"

"Yeah, earlier. He hasn't done any interviews and it's staying that way for the foreseeable future. He says he doesn't know what's going on any more than we do."

"Bullshit. Those are his boys. He was with them all the time." I park in front of the liquor store.

"I'm going to go visit this weekend if you wanna come with. Misty's coming along as well."

"Misty?" I blink. "You talk to her?"

"Sometimes."

"Why?" My voice erupts into something that sounds possessive even to my own ears, but I can't double down now. Besides, I don't want to. The last thing I need is for my brother to get between me and Misty, not that he would knowingly.

"Relax." Mav chuckles. "She's going to visit Jo this weekend and I wanted to see Jag. Rocky's coming too."

"Rocky, huh? Are you finally coming around to the fact that you're in love with her?"

"I'm not . . . " He lowers his voice. "She just got home. I gotta go."

"Fine. I'll talk to you tomorrow."

"Hey, Mitch," he calls out as I'm about to hang up.

"Yeah?"

"She doesn't date athletes," he says, "Misty. She's totally against dating an athlete."

"She told you that?"

"Her friend did. I was wearing my hockey uniform when I ran into them and I guess she thought I was trying to put the moves on Misty."

"Were you?"

"No." He laughs again. "She's like a sister to me."

"So was Rocky and here we are."

"Shut up." He groans. "I'm trying to help you out here. She doesn't want to date an athlete."

"We'll see. Count me in for the trip."

"Okay." Mav's voice is full of amusement.

I hang up and toss my phone in the passenger seat, shutting my eyes as I lay my head against the headrest. When I let Misty go the first time, I did it because it was the right thing to do, but I always assumed we'd get back together with her when my life was sorted out, when it wasn't so chaotic. I hadn't planned for her to be so opposed to the idea of dating an athlete. Or me.

Chapter Ten

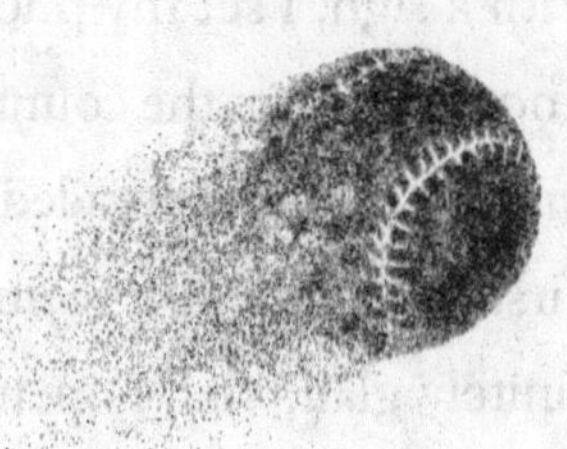

Misty

EXPECTED LOUD MUSIC IN THEIR APARTMENT, BUT IT'S PRETTY quiet as I walk into mine. When I shut the door and walk to the living room, I hear music though, and realize I'll probably hear it all night. It's fine. I can deal with that. Mitch's invitation was a surprise, but after considering it I reached the conclusion that it wasn't a good idea. A part of me wants to go and call it research, but I know him. He'll start flirting with me and then I'll get upset and wish I'd never gone at all. My muscles are aching from today's workout and the only thing I want to do right now is shower, put on my lounging clothes, have a glass of wine, and relax, so that's what I set out to do.

I'm scrolling social media and on my third glass of wine when the doorbell rings. With a sigh, I set my phone down and walk over, taking the money I set on the counter with me so that I can tip the delivery boy. I hadn't intended to order pizza tonight, but after my first glass of wine it seemed like a good idea and now I'm definitely glad I did. I open the door and blink at Mitchell, who's standing on the other side, with his left forearm pressed against the doorframe, showing off his toned arm in that short-sleeved polo shirt he's wearing. My pulse quickens at the gorgeous view. I shoo it away.

"I thought you were having a party?"

"Why aren't you there?"

"I never said I was going." I shrug a shoulder. "Besides, I'm busy."

"Busy doing what exactly?" His eyes search my face. "Are you having a spa night?"

"What?" I feel myself frown and realize I'm wearing stickers under my eyes. I reach up and pull them off quickly. "I'm just chillin' and waiting for a pizza."

"We have pizza."

"Good for you. So will I in about five minutes."

"We have drinks."

"I have wine."

"Wine?" He frowns. "What are you, thirty?"

I roll my eyes. "What are you, five?"

"Bring your wine." He shrugs. "We have music."

"I have a phone and a speaker."

"We have company."

"If everything is so grand over there then why the hell are you here?" I raise an eyebrow.

"Because you're not there." He pushes off the doorframe and stands straight, so I have to crane my neck to look into his green eyes. What I find in them makes me take a step back, letting go of the door as he takes a step forward to stop it from shutting.

"What are you doing?" My voice comes out breathless.

"I want you to come up to the party."

"I don't want to." I swallow. "I'm waiting for pizza."

"Okay." He nods a few times, glancing away as if trying to figure out what his next move will be. When he looks at me, I can tell he's solved the riddle playing inside his head. "Can I stay?"

"For pizza?"

"Sure."

"What about your party?" My heart pounds rapidly as we stare at each other.

"They can wait." He shrugs a shoulder, his eyes focused on mine in a way that sends my pulse racing.

"Did you order pizza?" a voice asks from the hall and I've never been more relieved for an interruption.

"Yes." I push between the doorframe and Mitchell and practically collide with the pizza box the delivery guy is handing over. I shove money into his hand and grab the box from him. "Thank you."

Turning back to my apartment, I find Mitch holding the door open for me. I try not to dwell on this. Not on the fact that he's here, his words, and how they made me feel. Not the way my head is swimming in wine and I need to get food into my system, or else. I walk inside and head to the kitchen, setting the box down and quickly searching for disposable plates. I have ceramic plates, but I forgot to buy dish cleaner and therefore, I'm sticking to disposable for now.

"I'm surprised you even own these." Mitch waves the disposable plate I set in front of him. "Miss Reduce, Reuse, Recycle."

"They were here when I moved in," I say and explain the dish soap situation.

"Ah, I'm sure we have extra."

"I'd appreciate it." I don't look at him as I serve us each a slice.

"Cheese, huh? Still with your cheese is the best topping you could ever ask for thing?"

"I never said that." I look at him now. "I said it's the easiest topping to judge a pie by. If you start adding toppings, you get lost in other flavors, so I stick to cheese."

"And?" He takes a bite after I do.

"It's good," I say when I'm finished chewing. "It's big."

"That's what she said." The side of his mouth turns up.

I shake my head and keep eating. When I'm done with my first slice, I start feeling a little less hazy, remember my manners, and ask him if he wants something to drink. He goes for wine, which surprises me.

"What are you, thirty?" I ask as I pour him a glass and slide it over to him, setting an elbow on the counter as I look up at him.

He chuckles. "I drink wine on special occasions."

"What's so special about this occasion?" I ask, then add, "And if you say me I swear I'll vomit."

Mitch chuckles as he takes a sip of wine. "In that case, I'll keep my mouth shut."

"Why are you here?" I straighten. "Really, why are you here?"

"I miss you." He sets his glass down and walks around the counter so he's in front of me. "I miss being with you."

"That's impossible, Mitchell," I whisper. "You were only with me for a moment."

"And a moment was all it took." He brings a hand up

and cups my face. "What can I do to convince you to give me another chance?"

"Nothing." I blink rapidly, silently praying I don't start to cry. Stupid wine. "I don't know that I can open myself up to you again."

"That's fair." He swallows. "Friends, then?"

"Friends." I eye him cautiously.

The sparkle in his green eyes does nothing to convince me that he truly means to stay in the friend zone, but I decide to go along with it for now.

Chapter Eleven

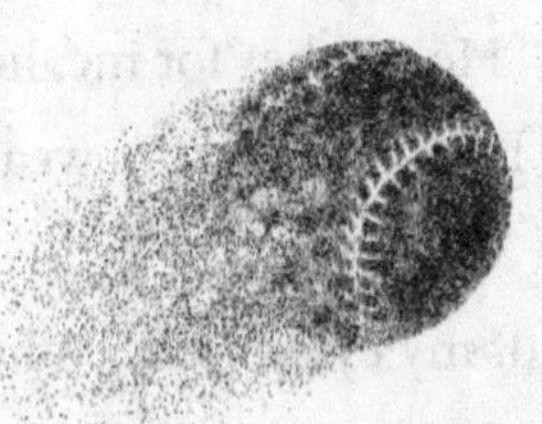

MY EYES POP OPEN AT THE SOUND OF THE DOORBELL. WHEN I look at the clock, it says five thirty. I shake my head and bury my face into my pillow. No freaking way. It rings again. I groan before getting out of bed and walking over to it slowly. Sure enough, it's Mitchell, looking all fresh faced and ready for a run.

"It's your day off." I open the door with a heavy sigh. "Why are you doing this to yourself?"

He chuckles. "Going on a run?"

"At five thirty in the morning."

"Early bird and all that."

"I'm not a bird and if I was, I certainly wouldn't be an early one. I'm tired. Go away." I start shutting the door, but he catches it with his hand and pokes his head inside.

"Come on, Misty. Don't you want as much information as you can get?"

"I already have it. You guys work way too hard and only a very low percentage gets to reap those benefits beyond college. I don't need to go on a five a.m. run for that."

"So go on the run with a friend just because."

I glare at him.

"Come on, Mist." He reaches for me, hooking a finger into the pocket of the light cardigan I'm wearing. "Keep me company."

"I hate you." I shut my eyes briefly. When I open them again, he looks like he's trying hard not to smile. "You're making me coffee while I get ready."

"I'm on it." He walks toward the kitchen as I head to my room and shut the door between us.

This is all too reminiscent of the first time we fell in love and it scares me, but because of our history, I do believe Mitchell when he says he wants to be just friends. Everyone knows baseball is his number one, first love, and everything and everyone else pales in comparison to how he feels about that. As long as I keep that in mind, I'll be fine.

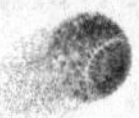

"You good?" Mitch asks.

I nod, unable to respond because I'm saving all of my

energy for breathing as I run. Today's run has been surprisingly easier than yesterday's, despite my aching muscles and the exhaustion I felt when I started. We're almost done and even though I've kept a very slow pace that Mitchell has graciously matched, it's been good. We slow down when we get to the tree we started by and I put my arms over my head, focusing on my labored breath. Mitch looks totally unfazed by this, which doesn't surprise me. My sister is like that as well. She's been doing it for so long that her body just responds with the motions and her lungs don't seem to get as worked up as a regular person.

"I guess I'm going to cancel Pilates for the week," I say when I feel I can speak again.

"You might as well."

"My mother won't be pleased."

"You can blame me." He winks. My heart does a little leap before I reel it in and remind it that we're not here to fall for him.

"She wouldn't even be upset if I blamed you." I roll my eyes. My mother loves Mitchell and his brothers.

"Yet another reason you should just stop playing around and give me a chance."

I lower my hands and start walking a little faster, ignoring his words. This is exactly why I knew from the beginning that this assignment was a bad idea for me to take. Following the baseball team around is one thing. Following

Mitchell around is just plain dumb. He's constantly making jokes like that and flirting with me and I can't handle it. I've become an expert at fielding his advances though, so I cling on to that and continue to ignore him. When we reach the apartment building, he holds the door open for me. We ride the elevator in silence, and when we reach our floor, I walk past his door and stop in front of mine, startled to find he's still beside me.

"Let's go grab something to eat."

"No." As if on cue, my stomach growls and I remember I don't have much in my apartment. "Fine, but you need to stop coming onto me."

"Fine. I'll see you in a few." He walks away and I walk into my apartment, shutting the door quickly behind me.

I don't even give myself a chance to overthink this as I head to the shower to get ready. I'm way too hungry and I have to keep my eye on the prize.

Chapter Twelve

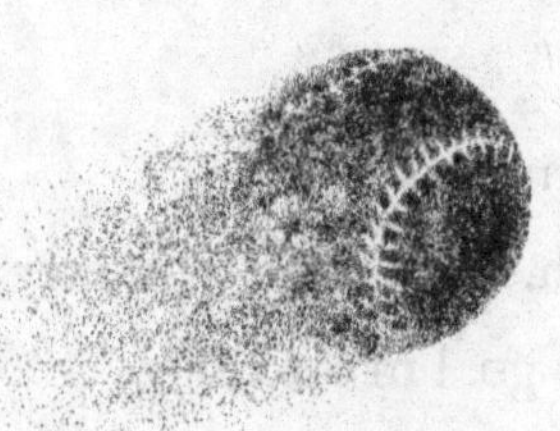

Mitch

MY PHONE RINGS AS MISTY AND I ARE GETTING IN THE CAR and even though I completely want to dodge Silvie's call, my Bluetooth picks it up.

"Oh my God. I'm shocked you answered," she says upon hearing the call go through. I take a deep breath and let it out as Misty buckles her seat belt beside me.

"I didn't. My car answered for me."

Misty's jaw drops as she glances over at me. I only look at her for a second before I put the car in reverse and start driving.

"I haven't seen you around in a while."

"Been busy."

"With baseball?" she asks. I roll my eyes. Obviously with baseball. What else? I decide not to indulge her with an answer. "I've been texting."

"I know, but I've been busy."

"I sent you a nude and you didn't even respond."

"Is that the reason for this call, Silvie?"

"I miss you."

"I'm sure you'll manage."

"Come on, Mitch." Her voice is quieter now.

"Listen, I have to go. I'm on a date."

"A date?" Silvie's voice rises again. "You don't go on dates."

"It appears that I do."

"That is so fucked up. I gave you a year of my life and you—"

"I didn't ask you to give me a year of your life."

"You told me you didn't go on dates or do the relationship thing."

"I don't."

"Yet you're on a date."

"Yes, and I'm keeping her waiting. I'm sure I'll see you around." I hang up the phone before she says anything else. As it is, divulging she sent me a nude was a bit much, but I don't sweat it. It's not like Misty is taking me seriously anyway.

"That was so rude," Misty says after a moment.

"What was?"

"That entire conversation. It's obvious that girl is into you and you were so mean to her."

"I'm not into her." I shrug a shoulder, glancing over at her. "And she doesn't seem to take a hint."

"But you were into her at one point." She crosses her arms and glances away, out the passenger window. "I don't know why I'm surprised."

"About what? Me not being into her or being rude?"

"The rude part." She shoots me a scathing look. "You want to be with people and once you decide it's over, your go-to move is to be unapologetically rude. It's an extremely unattractive trait."

"Oh, you're rating my traits now?" I try to sound nonchalant about it, but her words hurt and what's worse is that she's not wrong. I am mean when I decide I'm done with someone. My brothers point it out all the time.

"I don't care enough about you to rate your traits, period." She shrugs a shoulder.

"Ouch." I feel myself frown. "Speaking of mean."

"Yeah, well, I learned from the best." She meets my eyes again when I park in front of the restaurant. "Also, this isn't a date."

"You said we were going to go eat." I signal toward the restaurant.

"We are, but it's not a date."

"Just the two of us going out to eat?" I shoot her a look, raising my brow. "I'm calling it a date."

"You can call it whatever you want. You can even call it torture, but it's not a date." She gets out of the car and shuts the door. I let out a laugh and do the same, pushing the button to lock it as I meet her on the sidewalk.

"Was it because she said she sent me a nude?"

"Ew. No." She pulls a face as we head to the door. "I just don't want you to think this is something it's not."

"A friend date then?"

"Why do you have to label everything?"

"I don't label anything."

"Really? So you only like to label things with me then?" She walks inside when I hold the door open for her, but she's still looking at me as I speak to the hostess, waiting for an answer I can't give her, because she's right, I do label everything when it comes to her.

Chapter Thirteen

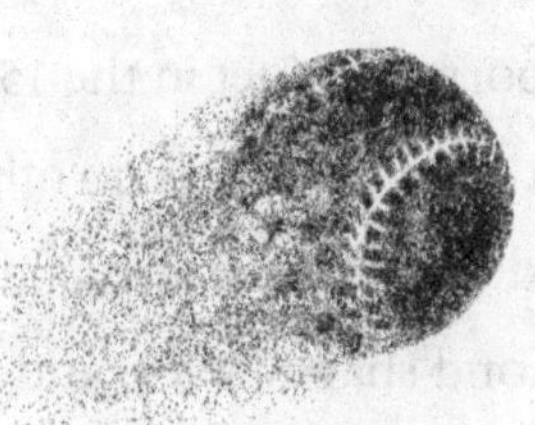

Past

Misty

MY PARENTS NEVER LET MY SISTER AND ME OUT OF THEIR sight, so it was a shock when they agreed to let me come to New York for the summer. It probably had a lot to do with the fact that my sister was going to a volleyball camp, and my parents were workaholics who didn't want to entertain me or watch me mope around the house. Nevertheless, I was overjoyed when they agreed to let me stay with my aunt Nini for a couple of months. Their agreement didn't come easily. Aunt Nini lived in the same apartment building as our family friends, The Cruzes, so if my aunt would be out for the night, she was to tell them to keep an eye on me. I was seventeen. I didn't need anyone to keep an eye on me, but my parents were strict, and I didn't even bother arguing. I couldn't keep the smile off my face as I walked outside of the airport and spotted my aunt.

She looked like a Taino Princess, or at least what I assumed one would look like. The Dominican Republic's indigenous people were reported extinct in the 1500s, and yet, if you looked at my aunt Nini, there was no other explanation for the matter. She had deep brown skin, a defined jawline, high cheekbones, almond-shaped eyes, and thick, straight, striking black hair. She had a look that said intense and wore bright colors to show it off even more so. My mother sometimes joked that I could pass as Aunt Nini's daughter, but I didn't have those super-defined curves or the confidence she carried them with.

Everyone in my family with the exception of Aunt Nini moved to North Carolina, but she always said New York made her feel like she was back home. Home, meaning the Dominican Republic. I always found it odd when she called it home since Aunt Nini moved to the United States when she was little. Despite our distance, we saw each other pretty often. Mom always said Aunt Nini was her best friend and that no amount of distance put between them could ever change that. When my aunt spotted me, her picture-perfect smile widened, and she shook her head as she walked over, wrapping her arms around me and pulling me into her warmth.

"I'm so happy you're here," she crooned against my hair.

"Me too. Thanks so much for letting me come."

"Are you kidding?" She pulled back slightly, taking me in. "I can't think of a better person to spend the summer with."

I smiled and let her help me with my bags. I tried to pack as light as possible, opting to bring a large suitcase and a small carry-on—an improvement from the two large suitcases I wanted to bring. As we walked to the car, Aunt Nini told me all about her life, primarily her dating life, which was always exciting. As we drove toward her apartment building in Chelsea, I took my camera out and snapped pictures of everything—the buildings, the sidewalks, the people. New York had always felt like it was calling for me, and I had always said that this was where I wanted to be.

She parked at the parking lot down the street, and we walked over to the building, greeting the doorman as he opened the door for us. As we rode the elevator, my aunt told me about the area and the eateries I'd find around here if I wanted to explore without her.

"I'll be honest, I'll be pretty MIA during the week," Aunt Nini said as we walked to her apartment.

"I know, don't worry, I don't require much attention." I shot her a smile. "I'll probably spend my days photographing anyway."

"I have a few big cases I'm working on right now and I need to focus on those, but every second of free time I get, I'll spend with you."

"I'm sure I'll be fine." I smiled.

"You can always hang out with the Cruz kids. They're up on the penthouse floor." She nodded up as she unlocked the door and swung it open. "I haven't spoken to Milly, but I'm sure the boys are home for the summer. I mean, when they're not playing sports. You know they don't stop practicing and training." She rolled her eyes. I laughed.

It was another thing Aunt Nini and I had in common. We didn't understand how people could be so obsessed with sports. My sister had been playing volleyball forever, and while I thought it was cool that she'd found something she was passionate about, I didn't understand why she spent so much time on fitness. She was either always running or playing. Of course, she might have been using it as an excuse to hang out with her friends and get my parents off her back.

Spending time with the Cruz kids, as my aunt called them, sounded like fun. We'd known each other our entire lives, but I hadn't seen them in a while. I made a note to knock on their door the next morning. If I was going to have this much free time here, I might as well spend it with native New Yorkers.

Chapter Fourteen

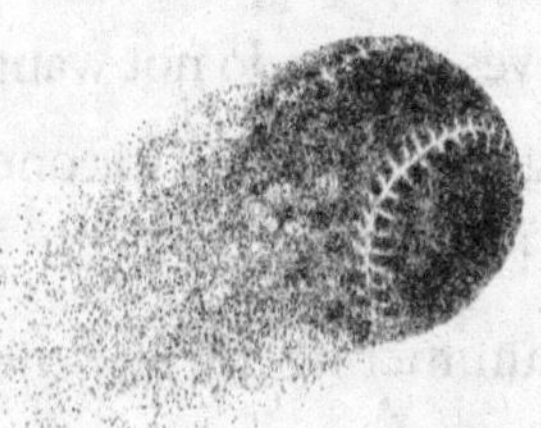

Present

Misty

"I FEEL LIKE I'VE APOLOGIZED A MILLION TIMES AND I CAN spend my life apologizing a million more, but that won't make a difference," Mitch says across from me. He ordered a stack of pancakes that stacks higher than my torso and he's been enjoying every bite, while I eat an açai bowl that looked amazing until I saw the stack of pancakes.

"I already forgave you." I stab my spoon into the bowl in front of me. "And I already told you I don't want to talk about it again."

"And I already told you that I do."

"It's not always about you, Mitchell." I shoot him an annoyed glance. "Get over yourself. If you can't let me do my job and write this article without bringing this up, then I'm just going to have to tell Valerie that I can no longer write it."

"Seriously?" His eyes widen. "You'd give this up because you hate me that much?"

"I don't hate you." I groan, bringing my hands up to my face and rubbing my eyes. "I just do not want to discuss our very short-lived dating life. We dated for one summer, you broke up with me, end of story."

"It was the best summer of my life," he says, so low I almost don't hear him. My heart does; it thrashes inside my chest as if awakened for the first time in years.

"Please don't say things like that." I look up and meet his gaze.

"It's the truth, Mist. For years I've been lying, trying not to even breathe too hard around you because everything I do bothers you, but I can't not speak the truth." His lips form a small smile that's almost shy, very unlike Mitchell. "I'll try to keep my thoughts and feelings hidden away for the sake of your assignment though."

"Thank you." I swallow and look at my bowl again. "How's baseball going?"

"Fine."

"Oh. I have a question." I look up again, this time putting aside all of my tumultuous feelings and focusing on my assignment. "How do you feel about collegiate athletes not getting paid?"

Mitch chuckles. "Like shit. How else would I feel?"

"True. Do you think that's the reason so many athletes started selling and distributing drugs on the side?"

"Maybe." He cuts the pancakes and puts a chunk in his mouth, chewing slowly. He looks uncomfortable answering, which really fuels my curiosity.

"Did you know any of the guys?" I ask, lowering my voice.

He shrugs, still chewing.

"Jagger definitely knew some of them. Most were football players."

Another shrug.

"So you do know."

"I'll tell you a secret if you drop the questions about this." He takes a sip of water and sets it down. I lean forward a little because I have no chill when I hear the word *secret*. "There's a lot of talk right now about this thing called NIL. The NCAA is discussing it right now and if they come to an agreement, college athletes will finally be able to get paid real money."

"What?" I frown. "Like the college is going to pay them? As if they were employees?" I put a hand up quickly. "Which, you are. I'm not going to argue that. I know they make billions of dollars and you guys don't get paid which is the reason we're in this situation in the first place."

"Right, but no, the schools are going to pay us. It's . . . " He moves his stack of pancakes to the side and sighs as he leans back against his side of the booth. "I'm trying to figure out a way to explain it because the way my dad explained it to me sounded complicated, but basically, let's say a company wanted to pay me for a sponsorship, I would get paid and walk around drinking, eating, or wearing whatever it was they paid me for."

"Like Lebron and Jordan."

"Exactly, but while still playing college ball. Lebron was able to do that because he went from high school straight to the NBA and didn't have to deal with the four years of unpaid . . . internship, let's call it."

"So basically, you're monetizing your name while playing in college."

"Yep."

"Do you consider playing for UNC an unpaid internship?"

"Isn't that what it is?"

"I mean, I guess." I shrug. "I've never really thought about it."

He sets the pancakes in front of him and dives right in again. I focus on my açai bowl. After a moment, I look up at him. His eyes meet mine not even a split second after I look at him and once again I have to swallow back this yearning I can't seem to kick.

"So." I lick my lips. "Do you think the student athletes that got in trouble for selling and distributing will get somewhat of a break in light of this new NIC thing?"

"NIL." Mitch chuckles. "It's NIL. And I don't know. This hasn't gone through yet. It's not official."

"When do you think it will be official?"

"Soon. Unfortunately for my brother, not soon enough. He'll probably be out of here before me at this rate." He shakes his head, eyes back on his pancakes.

"Does that bother you?"

Another shrug.

I sigh and finish eating my bowl in silence. It's obvious he's not going to talk about the arrests and I'm not going to keep pushing him to. It's not like I have to. I have an entire lineup at my disposal that I can question.

Chapter Fifteen

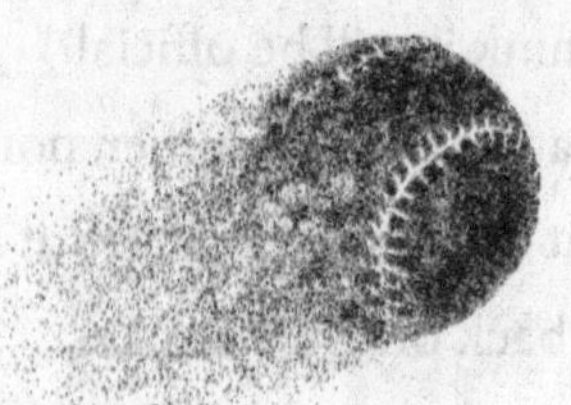

DYLAN OPENS THE DOOR TO THEIR APARTMENT AND I WALK in quietly, notepad in one hand, cup carrier with four Frappuccinos in the other. Dylan relieves me of the cup carrier and thanks me as he walks into the kitchen and I shut the door behind me. Mitchell's voice is boisterous and animated as I walk farther into the apartment and find three of the baseball players and Maverick in the living room, watching Mitchell as he demonstrates some type of pitching form. I lean against the wall and watch along, without disturbing. This is what I wanted, to be a fly on the wall, immersed in their element without them noticing me. It's the only way to write an authentic story on them.

"So you're propelling the ball with your hips," Maverick says.

"No." Mitch sighs heavily, running a hand through his hair. "Pay attention." Mitch is setting up his stance again. "I'm here, right? My arm is back here. Then, when I'm about to let go of the ball, I point my toe this way, and pivot my hips, so the momentum is coming from my back leg, right here." He slaps his hamstring. "And then I let go."

"Bro, you're telling me this would work on any ball I throw?" Mav frowns.

"What balls are you throwing?" Rodney asks with a chuckle. "You only know how to swing a hockey stick."

"Fuck you. I played baseball and hockey in high school." Mav raises an eyebrow. "I have a mean arm."

"He does," Mitchell responds, almost grumbling.

"If that's the case, why'd you stick with hockey?" Dylan asks, walking over to them with the cup carrier. They pluck the Frappuccinos out of the holder and only then does Mitchell look back and see me, his green eyes alighting with surprise and something that makes warmth pool in my stomach.

"How long have you been standing there?" he asks.

"Long enough to have learned a thing or two about throwing the ball hard."

"Faster," Mitchell says, lopsided smile on his face

that makes my blood pulse. "I'm glad you're learning something."

"You should write something about me in that article you're working on," Maverick says, slurping on the Frap. "And Rocky. I bet she'll let you follow her around."

"She's only focusing on athletes who are in the thick of it," Mitch says. "And you're about to go pro."

"You could go pro too." Maverick shoots him a look. "I hate when you use that jealous tone of yours like you can't be playing in the majors right now."

"I can't."

"It's too early for this conversation." Maverick leans back on the couch and sighs. "Anyone else get tired of this guy's whining?"

Dylan and Rodney chuckle but don't say anything and I remain quiet because I've seen these two brothers come to blows once or twice and I'd rather not feed into it.

"Is practice canceled today?" I ask because they're all sitting around like they have nothing to do.

"Yep. All week," Rodney says. "We're going to have an unofficial practice later though. Six."

I groan. "I can't go at six."

"Why? What do you have going on?" Mitch asks.

"Work."

"Are we still on for this weekend?" Maverick asks.

"Definitely." I smile. "Rocky is still on board, right?"

"Yeah, she's going."

"As am I," Mitch adds.

"Cool." I try to sound as nonchalant as possible.

"How's your school handling all this?" Mav asks.

"I mean, I'm writing an article on your school's athletes, so I'd say they're trying to bury it under the rug?" I let out a laugh.

"Right, let us take the fall."

"I mean, most of the athletes were in your school, so . . ."

"Bullshit. You know this goes from here up to Ellis, right?" Mav asks. "I wouldn't be surprised if it started in Ellis."

"Sketchy bastards," Dylan says.

"I'm surprised you didn't go to Ellis," Rodney says to me. "You transferred from NYU, right?"

"Yeah, and I don't have a death wish."

"You believe all those rumors?" That's Dylan.

"About the missing girls and the secret societies?" I blink. "Uh, yeah."

"You believe them?" He glances at Mitch, Maverick ,and Rodney, who all nod.

"I have a couple of friends in secret societies up there," Maverick says, then shoots me a look. "Don't get any ideas because I'm not giving you any names."

"That's fine." I laugh. "I wouldn't want them anyway.

Like I said, I value my life. I have enough anxiety without having to worry about getting kidnapped and killed."

"Fair point." Mav slaps his legs as he stands up. "I'll see you guys later."

"What do you have going on right now?" Mitch asks.

"Rocky's at the park and practice is canceled for me too so I figured I'd go practice with her."

"Soccer too, huh?" Dylan says. "You're just good at everything with a ball then?"

"Yup. Especially these two." Mav grabs himself with both hands. I shake my head as we all laugh. He smiles and straightens. "Sorry, Mist. They just don't stop trying me, you know?"

"It's fine." I shrug a shoulder. "I'll walk out with you."

"You're leaving too?" Mitch asks.

"Yep. I have to catch up on homework before I go to work." I flash a smile. "Bye, guys."

Mav and I walk out of the apartment talking about our impending trip. He wants to go visit Jagger and I want to go visit my sister.

"You're okay with this assignment? Having to see my brother all the time?"

"Yeah." I sound as surprised as I feel. Mitchell's and my relationship is something we've never openly discussed with anyone. As far as I knew, only my sister was privy to that information, but it makes sense that his brothers would know as well.

"Okay, because if you need other UNC athletes to follow around, you know where you can find us."

"Thanks, Mavy." I kiss his cheek when he leans down to say goodbye and I walk into the apartment next door.

Chapter Sixteen

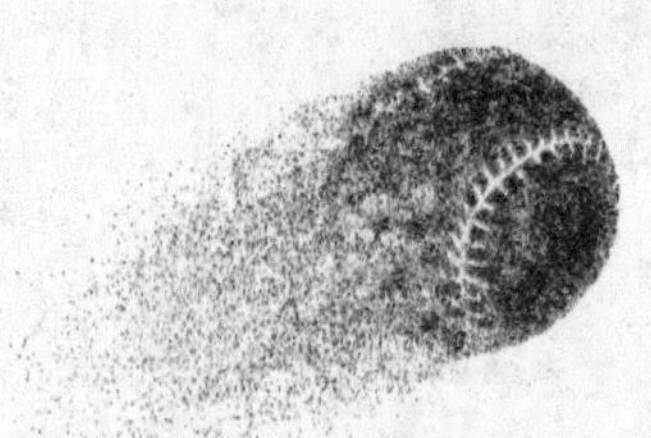

'M EXHAUSTED FROM YESTERDAY'S OVERWHELMING SHIFT AT THE coffee shop, and even more exhausted from my mind running all night. I was fully intending to sleep in, but when I hear the doorbell, I immediately know it's time for the morning run. *Not today, Mitchell.* It's what I tell myself over and over as I brush my teeth and get a robe, and what I greet him with as soon as I open the door and find him on the other side of it, dressed in workout shorts and a T-shirt that I can tell he turned into a muscle tank top.

"What do you mean not today? Yes today."

"No. I'm tired." I yawn. "Like seriously tired."

"So am I."

"I'm not the athlete. You are." I let go of the door and

walk away, not even bothering to stop in the kitchen to make myself coffee. I am not going today.

"So?"

"So, I'm not the one getting paid for my NIL or whatever."

He chuckles behind me. "Nice. I'm not either. I already told you, it's not official yet."

"Just as well. I'm not going." I climb back into bed, robe and all, and pull the comforter up.

Instead of leaving, he walks to the other side of the bed and plops down with a sigh.

"Seriously?" I turn on my side and look at him.

"Your bed is comfortable. More comfortable than mine."

"Take it up with your parents. Didn't they furnish these apartments?"

"Yep." He yawns, eyes closed. "Maybe we can take a nap and run when we wake up."

"Maybe you should go run by yourself. I'm not interested."

"I'm not interested in running by myself."

"Well, you have two roommates."

"Nope." He opens his eyes and meets mine. "I want you to go with me."

"How'd you get in my bed anyway? I didn't invite you."

"You want me to leave?"

"Not really." I shrug. "As long as you don't try anything stupid."

"And get kicked out for good?" He chuckles. "I wouldn't dream of it."

I wait for him to close his eyes and then I do the same. It's comforting having him here. Very reminiscent of that summer we shared together, the one that changed everything between us.

Chapter Seventeen

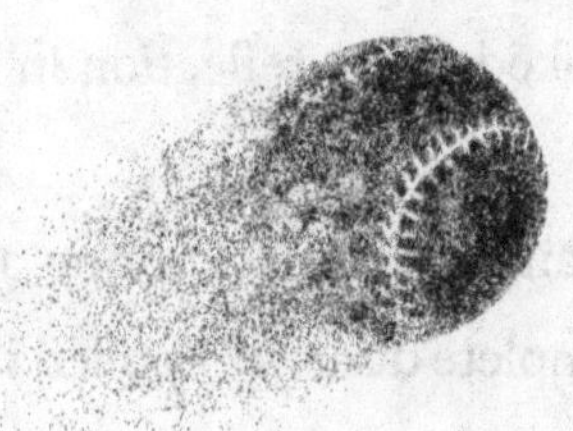

Misty

HERE WAS A KNOCK ON THE DOOR, QUICKLY FOLLOWED BY THE sound of the doorbell, that woke me up from a nap. I yawned as I got out of bed, pulling the long, thin robe closed. I was wearing short shorts and a tank top underneath. It wasn't like I was in lingerie or naked, but still. Through the peephole, I saw Mitchell Cruz. My eyes widened. I hadn't seen him since last year, and as I opened the door, I swore he'd grown at least a foot taller. He grinned as I came into view, and my heart stuttered.

"Second day here and you're napping?" His green eyes gleamed mischief as he spoke.

"I wasn't napping. I was resting my eyes." My brows furrowed as I stepped back, letting him into the apartment. "How'd you know I was napping anyway?"

"Your hair's a mess." He patted the top of my head and walked in with ease and comfort like he owned the place. I shut the door and looked at my reflection in the long mirror beside me.

My loose ponytail had come undone and my long, brown hair was in complete disarray. I pulled the elastic and fixed it. My cheeks were slightly pink and I wasn't sure if it was from my interaction with Mitch or my nap. I looked like I was wearing light blush on my naturally olive, currently makeup-less skin. I stopped primping and followed Mitch into the living room. He had gotten taller. He was probably six foot three now. At five foot seven, I had to crane my neck to look at him, and for comparison, my father was six foot one, so I knew Mitch had to be right around that height. He'd filled out some as well, his tanned muscular arms a lot more defined. He was wearing a sleeveless workout T-shirt and shorts.

"What are you doing here anyway?" I asked.

"I was going to ask you if you wanted to go for a run."

"A run?" My eyes widened. "What in the world would make you think I'd want to run on purpose?"

"Aw, come on, Misty. You run."

"Not on purpose." I blinked. "I'm not my sister."

"But you can run, right?" His words were a bit slower, as if he needed to make sure of this before he asked again.

"Yes, but I don't enjoy it."

"Not even in Central Park? It's beautiful there. You'd love it."

"Can we walk in Central Park?" I crossed my arms.

"Sure, let's go for a walk then." He chuckled and I was sure I'd die then.

"When did you get hot?" I blurted out, then slapped my forehead.

Mitchell laughed harder. "When did you?"

"I've always been hot." I shrugged.

"Really?" His eyes were full of mischief. "And I haven't?"

"Not particularly. You were always lanky and tall, but not . . . not hot."

"Well, then, I'm glad you think I'm hot now."

"I mean, I don't see why that matters. I'm just making an observation."

"I'm glad you're making it," he said, and I could tell he was trying not to laugh at me.

"So, I guess I'll go get ready for that walk?" I said awkwardly, walking toward the guest room I was staying in.

"Yep. I'll be right here," he said. "Where's your aunt anyway?"

"She's working on a big case. She told me to go upstairs and knock on your door, but I didn't want to intrude," I called out as I changed into the only pair of athletic shorts I brought, a sports bra, and sneakers. It would have to do. I'd only packed this in case I got bored and decided to go to Pilates with Aunt Nini, and even though that wasn't happening, I was glad to be putting it to use.

"That sucks," he said. He was facing the window when I walked out into the living room and turned around when he heard my squeaky sneakers. His eyes widened. "You were right."

"About what?"

"You were always hot." He cocked his head. "Scratch that. Beautiful. You've always been beautiful."

My heart skipped a beat and I felt myself blush furiously. This was new, this feeling. I'd had crushes on guys before, but I'd never had this reaction to one when they told me I was hot. Then again, none of them had ever told me I was beautiful.

Chapter Eighteen

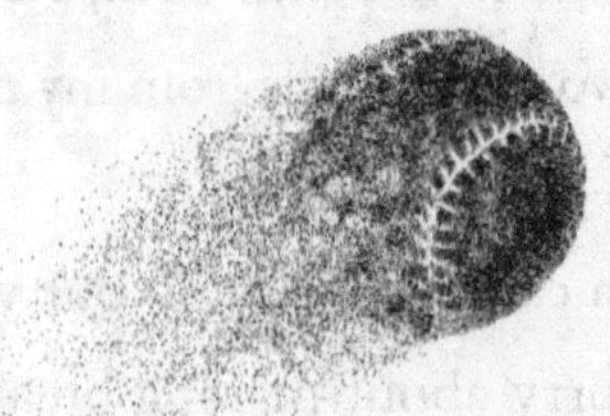

Present

Misty

I WAKE WITH A START, EYES POPPING OPEN QUICKLY. AT FIRST, I'M not sure what woke me, but then I feel it again, a foot on mine, and I remember. Mitchell's here. My heart skips a beat, then another, as I look over at him. Mitchell Cruz is sound asleep beside me in my bed. It's the stuff of my teenage fantasies for sure. When we dated, I dreamed of days like this, when we were old enough to share a bed with no judgement. Of course, my parents would definitely still judge. I'm pretty sure my father still thinks that I'm saving myself for marriage. It's that thought that makes me sit up straight in bed with a gasp. My parents. I start nudging Mitch.

"Wake up." I put both hands on his arm and shake him. "Mitch. You have to wake up right now."

"Hm."

"I'm serious! My parents are coming over." I get out of bed quickly and head to the bathroom, picking up my phone on the way. Two missed calls from my mother. I hit her name to call back. "Fuck."

"Misty! I've been calling. We're on our way to your apartment. Don't worry about making breakfast, we're bringing bagels, coffee, and donuts."

"Okay." I start rushing, picking up clothes from the floor and tossing it into the hamper. "What's your ETA?"

"Hmmmm . . . what's our ETA?" she asks my father, and I start to panic a little more because of the seriousness of this. Mitch needs to get the heck out here now. Then she adds, "Eight minutes."

"Okay. I'll see you when you get here." I hang up the phone and rush back into the room. "Mitchell. You need to get up."

He stirs and sits up when he hears my shout, rubbing his eyes and blinking rapidly at the sight of me, but not for long. I rush into the bathroom and turn on the shower. I'll have to take two minutes and skip out on washing my hair.

I'm in and out of the shower, wrapping the towel around myself when I hear the knock on the bathroom door.

"Why are you rushing?"

"You need to leave. I'll see you later." I finish drying, pull on my panties, and throw on the black flowy minidress with the little flowers before pulling my hair into a sleek bun and putting on some mascara.

It's not like I have to impress my parents, but I kind of do. I'm their problematic child, not because I do heavy drugs or party hard, but because my sister is a saint so next to her I'm automatically the wild one. Josephine lost her scholarship and got kicked off the volleyball team last year, and she's still the good, responsible one in comparison to me. It's ridiculous. It also makes my life a little easier since I don't have to prove that I'm great at everything all the time. And yet, I'm somehow always chasing that. So, yeah, cute little dress and nice sleek bun. When I open the door, I find Mitchell walking around my room.

"Dude. I told you to leave." I walk around the bed and grab the black combat boots my sister gave me last Christmas, pulling them on.

"You look nice."

"Mitch. You need to leave. Please. I'm begging you."

"Why?" He scowls. "You have a date or something?"

"If I say yes will you leave?"

"No." His scowl deepens. "Who is it?"

"Even if I told you a name, how the hell would you know who it is?"

"I probably wouldn't." His eyes narrow. "Unless he's on my team. Is it Dylan?"

"What? No." I stand up quickly. "My parents are coming over!"

"Oh. So why do I have to leave?"

"Don't you see how this looks?" I blink. "You and me alone in my apartment this early in the morning?"

"It's not like we did anything."

"It doesn't matter. They'll think something is up."

"Why is that such a bad thing? Is it because it's me?"

"It has nothing to do with you, Mitchell." I sound as exasperated as I feel. I start to shoo him with both hands. "Please. Come on."

"Your parents love me."

"Can you please just go?" I walk a little faster toward the door. "My anxiety is climbing every second you're still here and I'm trying to cut back on the medicinal marijuana, so I really need to keep it under control."

"Yeah, I heard about that." He searches my eyes. "I wish you didn't feel the need to depend on it."

"On what?" I blink. "Mitchell. Get out please. Jesus Christ. We can have this conversation later and you can judge all you want, but for the love of God, please."

"You're right. I'll be here at seven." He opens the door and stands in the hall.

"What?"

"Tonight. Seven o'clock. I'm coming over and we'll Netflix and chill."

"What? Fuck no. I'm not having sex with you."

"So we won't." His eyes get a little brighter, the way they do when he's really up to no good. My heart skips a beat. "We'll just actually just chill."

"Hm." My mouth turns up slightly. "How many girls do you actually just chill with?"

"Currently none."

"Somehow, I doubt that." I cross my arms, raising an eyebrow.

"Hey." My mom's voice rings out in the hallway. Mitchell turns toward her and I stick my head out to watch as she and my dad walk toward us. They have huge smiles pointed at Mitch. "Your mom told me you were living next door. How are you?" She sets down the bags in her hand and hugs him.

"I'm doing well. I was trying to get this one to go for a run with me, but she was all dressed up when I got here." He tells it so seamlessly, this lie, that even I find it hard to question. "Let me help you get these." He reaches down for the bags and gives my dad a sideways hug as my mother walks over to kiss my cheek.

I walk back into my apartment, holding the door for my

dad, who also stops to kiss my cheek on the way in, bags in his hands as well, as he talks to Mitchell, and I realize he'll be stuck here now. That was not part of the plan, but there's very little I can do, so I'm going to have to roll with it, the way I often have had to through the years after that summer. That's the problem with our parents being friends.

Chapter Nineteen

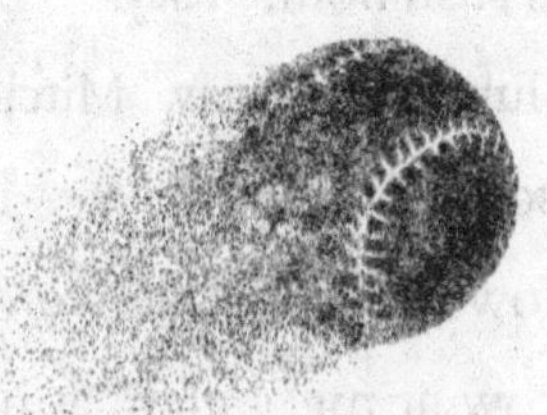

"**D**ID YOU GUYS BRING MY GROCERIES FOR THE WHOLE month?" I take in the things they're emptying out of the bags and storing for me.

"Don't we always?" Mom shoots me a look, then looks at Mitchell. "This one doesn't eat unless she's fed, it's almost like we're still spoon-feeding her."

"That's not true."

"Really? What have you had today?" She turns her back and places a carton of orange juice in the fridge.

"Nothing, but that's because we're supposed to have breakfast together."

"Right, and if we hadn't scheduled breakfast with you, I bet you wouldn't have consumed anything."

"She only eats when she's at the coffee shop, and barely,"

Dad adds. "I've held meetings there because the coffee is so good. Have you tried the coffee?" he asks Mitch, who shakes his head before dad continues, "It's phenomenal. Last meeting lasted two hours. When I got there she was nibbling on a muffin, when I left half of the muffin was still there."

"That's because I was working and you were there during lunch, which is rush hour," I say.

"We went out to lunch yesterday," Mitch says, "and she ate all her food. And some of mine."

I glare at him. Now it sounds like we were on a date. Mom raises an eyebrow at me. I glare at her as well, but it's short-lived because the subject is changed once more and while Dad and Mitchell continue putting away the groceries and start talking about baseball, Mom and I work on making breakfast. Throughout, I glance over and look at Dad and Mitch and find his eyes on me multiple times. The butterflies in my stomach are fluttering non-stop and I have to remind myself once again that this guy broke my heart and doesn't deserve it back. I'm all for forgiving people. I'm all for giving second chances. Unless your name is Mitchell Cruz. That's where I draw the line. I may be a lot of things, but an idiot is not one of them. The four of us take the food over to the table, which is small, but fits the four of us, and start eating.

"Dad, can you give up the baseball talk for five

seconds?" I ask. "I'm sure Mitchell is tired of thinking about that sport."

"I doubt it," Dad says.

"I'm not." Mitch chuckles. "I probably should be, and some days I definitely question whether or not I'm cut out for it, but it's all I know." He shrugs a shoulder.

"Do you think you'll graduate?" Mom asks in her Dean of Education voice that I hate when discussing my own education.

"Please. He could've gone pro without attending college," Dad says. It's the first I'm hearing of this.

"Why didn't you?" I glance at Mitch.

"Injury."

"Hm." I drop it because I can tell he doesn't want to talk about it, but I make it a point to ask him later. For the story, of course.

"How's the story coming along?" Mom asks me.

"It's . . . going," I say, because I don't want to get into the fact that I haven't even started writing the story.

"How much of it do you have done?" Dad asks. "When can we read it?"

"Not much." I sigh, taking a sip of the apple juice in front of me. "I kind of have writer's block right now."

"Oh." Mom frowns. "I thought you could only have writer's block if you were a fiction writer. I wasn't aware that was a thing amongst journalists."

"Well, apparently it is." I feel myself scowl, so I go back to my food.

"I'm sure it'll be great," Dad says, all cheerful. "Have you interviewed any players?"

"I have, and I follow them around a lot so they're in their element."

"She's been running with me at five thirty in the morning," Mitchell says. "So I can fully attest to the fact that she's committed."

"Hopefully committed enough to stay out of parties," Mom adds.

"I'm going to a party tonight in hopes that it'll help cure my writer's block." I grin.

"What party?" Mitch asks.

"A party. You don't have to know which one."

"I thought we were going to Netflix and chill."

"So you've been hanging out a lot then," Mom says, looking between Mitch and me. I feel my cheeks flame. I don't know what his reaction is because I refuse to look.

"Yeah, well, this assignment, you know." I shrug a shoulder.

"Do you go out to eat with all the players?" Dad asks.

"Not yet, but I was actually talking to Dylan about maybe grabbing dinner one of these days."

"When?" Mitch looks at me. Again, I refuse to look at

him, but I can feel his eyes burning a hole through the side of my face.

"One of these days," I say.

"Hm."

We finish having breakfast and Mitch excuses himself to go work out shortly after. Dad walks over to the couch and starts typing up something on his phone and Mom wastes no time in interrogating me.

"Are you dating?"

"What?" My jaw drops. "No freaking way."

"Misty." She shoots me a look.

"Sorry. But still, no way."

"He obviously has a thing for you."

"I'm hot and he's a guy." I roll my eyes.

Mom laughs. "So humble."

"Humility didn't do anything for Jo." I shrug a shoulder. "Except get her kicked off the volleyball team and grounded by you guys."

"That wasn't humility, that was stupidity." Mom shakes her head. "Thankfully she's doing very well now."

"Yeah, because she stopped being so humble and caring what others think of her and started living."

"Right." Mom laughs. "Back to Mitchell, though, it looks like he has a crush on you. I mean, for years we've known he has, but now it seems like he may just do something about it."

"Mom."

"What? I'm just stating facts." She smiles wide.

I roll my eyes. "A relationship between Mitchell and me will never happen, so you and your bestie should stop planning our wedding."

"Sure thing." Mom keeps smiling.

Dad's snore captures our attention and she finally drops it, but if I know my mother, I know this won't be the last time she asks.

Chapter Twenty

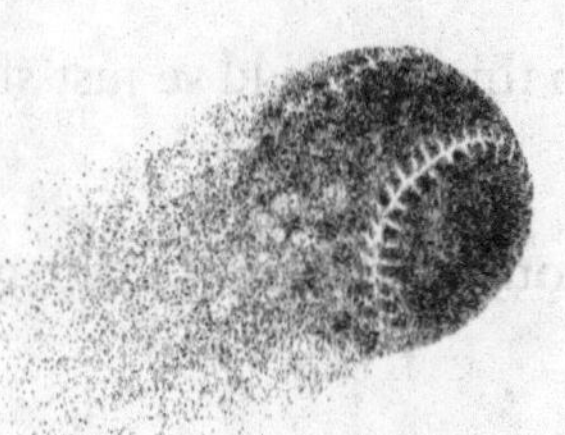

'M FINISHING UP MY MAKEUP WHEN MY SISTER CALLS ME ON A FaceTime. I answer and stand the phone up against the counter.

"What's up?"

"Damn. Where are you going?" she asks, eyeing my tight green miniskirt and the pink bralette I'm wearing as a shirt.

"A party with Soleil."

"Whose party?"

"Damon. Some guy she knows." I shrug. "I think he's a pre-med major."

"Ha. You just love those pre-med parties."

I stick my tongue out at her as I lift the phone in my hand and look at her. "You look nice. Where are you going?"

"Dinner with some of the players and their wives."

"Are they nice?"

"Very nice, actually."

"Good. How are things with the clinic coming along?"

"Slowly," she says, dragging the word.

"What happened now?"

"Nothing. I'm waiting on the inspectors again." She sighs. "Owning a business kind of sucks. I don't know why I let Dad talk me into this. I should've just stayed full-time with the team."

"It'll be so good once you get it off the ground, Jo."

"I know."

"You're so good at what you do. Everyone says it."

"Thanks." She doesn't sound like she believes me, but at least she's smiling. "So I heard you and Mitchell are dating?"

"What?" I let out a laugh. "Let me guess, Mom told you."

"She did."

"What did you say?"

"Nothing. I laughed and laughed some more." My sister smirks at me. "You know you're going to cave, right? You've been ignoring him and fending off his advances for a while, but now? Forget it."

"Forget what?" I shoot her a look. "I am single and enjoying the heck out of it."

"Right. Until you're not."

"I don't see that happening in the foreseeable future."

"Okay. I'll quote you on that."

"Okay." I stick my tongue out at her.

"So . . ."

"So?" I frown at my sister's cat-ate-the-canary face. My heart stops. "Don't tell me you're pregnant."

"What?" She starts laughing, then points the camera at Jagger, who's driving her.

"Hey, Jag."

"She's not pregnant. Yet," he says, raising an eyebrow.

"Not for a while." My sister shoots him a stern look, then looks at me in the camera again. "Jag and I are on our way there."

"What?" I squeal. "Really?"

"Yep." She smiles wide.

"Jo invited herself over to your parents' house this week-end," Jagger says.

"Why would you do that?" I frown. "You didn't even want to live there when you were in this town."

Jag chuckles. "That's what I said."

"Am I not allowed to miss my family?" she asks. "Besides, you ditched the plan to come see us this weekend."

"I didn't ditch the plan. Mav ditched it. He said his sched-uled moved."

"Well, go to Mom's house," Jo says.

"Tomorrow. At what time do you get here? Maybe you

can come to the party, or are you too cool for that now that you're a college graduate and shit?"

"We're tired. Besides, Jag needs to lay low."

"This is a Duke party. No one cares about Jagger."

"Oh, that's fucked up, Misty," Jagger says. "They cared about me when they went home crying after I kicked their ass my last game."

"Yeah, yeah." I roll my eyes. "But come to the party. I'll text you the address."

"I'm tired, but maybe," Jo says. "I'll text you when we get to Mom's."

"'Kay. Love you guys. See you tomorrow, and hopefully tonight."

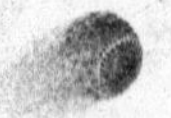

"You should've just packed a bag," Soleil says beside me. We're sipping on seltzer drinks as we people-watch from the sidelines. The party is pretty crowded thus far. "My place is much closer than yours. We can walk from here. My roommate is out of town anyway."

"All the more reason for me not to stay over. Archer's coming tonight, you know." I wink.

"Oh stop. Stop trying to make something out of nothing." She blushes.

"Is it nothing, though?" I raise an eyebrow.

"It's less of a thing than you and Mitchell." She raises an eyebrow right back.

"I hate everyone in my life." I sigh, drinking. "Mitchell and I are nothing."

"Hey, Mistyyyyy," a familiar male voice says. I look over in time to see Kian from . . . one of the classes I had last semester though I'm not sure which. I only remember his name because he introduced himself to me on three different occasions.

"Hey, Kian." I smile. "How are you?"

"Doing well. I heard you're working with traitors."

"Oh God. Here we go." I laugh because the rivalry never ceases to amaze me. "Where did you hear that?"

"Oh, you know. Word travels." He winks. I smile, but stop when my phone buzzes in my crossbody.

"Sorry, this is probably my sister." I pull out my phone with my free hand as Soleil and Kian start talking. I frown when I see that it's a text from Mitchell.

Mitch: He's lame.

My head snaps up. I look around the room and find Mitchell standing directly on the other side of the house, by the kitchen, leaning against the wall as women flank him and his friends. My heart stutters. Stupid. Stupid. Stupid. In an effort not to focus on his face, I look down at his shirt. My mouth falls open and I go back to my phone.

Me: You wore a UNC shirt to a Duke party!?!?!?!?!?!

Mitch: Lol yup.

Me: Wow.

I look back up at him, shaking my head. He's staring at me, but still typing. My phone buzzes a second later.

Mitch: Lose the guy, come get with me.

My heart comes full stop. And then starts again. I focus on breathing and my response and realize I have no response. After another second, I look up at him and start typing on my phone.

Me: You're the one with a gaggle of girls.

Mitch: None of them are you tho.

Me: You seriously need to give up flirting with me.

Mitch: Why would I when you're so close to falling?

I laugh so loud I wouldn't be surprised if he can hear me over the music and talking.

Me: Dream on.

This time, I put my phone in my bag. I chance one more glance in his direction and catch his eyes once more before one of the women next to him throws her arms around his neck and beckons his attention. I'd be lying if I said the sight of it didn't bother me, but I looked away and continued talking to Soleil and Kian anyway. Later, Soleil goes to the bathroom and I walk over to where the drinks are and find Archer there.

"Hey." He smiles at me and looks around.

"She's in the bathroom."

His shoulders drop slightly and he exhales like he's relieved.

"What?"

"Nothing. Just. I don't know where we stand right now." He takes a sip of his newly open beer. "Did she say anything to you?"

"About what?"

"I think I messed things up."

"How?" I frown, then turn to the table and grab another seltzer, opening it and taking a sip. "She seems like she likes you."

"I kind of assumed she was inviting me in when I dropped her off the other day, so I made to walk inside and she stopped me. I don't know. Maybe I'm reading into it because I'm so embarrassed for even thinking that." His light eyebrows pull in, making him look like a Precious Moments doll.

"Arch." I touch his arm. "I bet you didn't mess up at all. She's looking forward to seeing you tonight."

"Really?"

"Yes, really." I raise my eyebrows. "Would I lie to my boss?"

He chuckles. "I don't know about your boss, but I hope you wouldn't lie to a friend."

"That too." I smile.

"Austin told me you two decided to remain friends."

"Yep." I drop my hand from his arm and continue drinking. "I tried."

"Did you though?" He raises an eyebrow. "I know you're working with your ex."

"This has nothing to do with him."

"If you say so." He shrugs a shoulder. My phone buzzes in my purse again. I get it quickly in case it's Soleil. It's not.

Mitch: I don't like him.

I roll my eyes, not even bothering to look around for him this time.

Me: I didn't ask.

Mitch: He's not your type.

Me: Let me guess, you are.

Mitch: Stop rolling your eyes.

Me: Stop texting me. Go have fun with that blonde who clearly wants to fuck you. Don't forget, I know you. Once you get what you have, you disregard it without a second thought.

I turn off my phone and put it away again.

"You okay?" Archer asks. "You seem pissed."

"I'm fine." I smile wide even though I'm not feeling it. "Never better."

And then I proceed to drink until I feel it.

Chapter Twenty-One

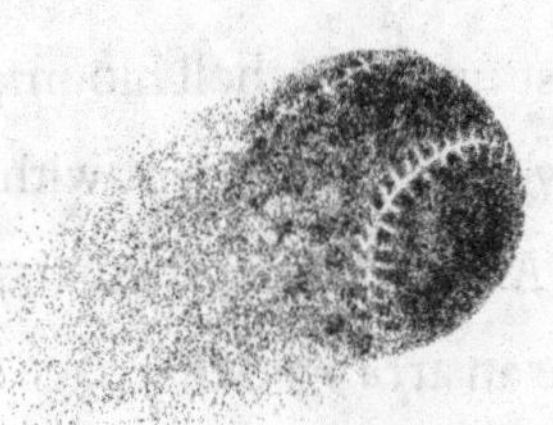

Past

WE WERE STANDING ON A ROOFTOP, DRINKING WATER WITH lime, not because I was opposed to underage drinking, but because the Cruz brothers were sticklers about it. They didn't drink, smoke, or have sugar. Their workouts were rigorous and their diets were immaculate, tailored to each one of their bodies and sports. I always knew that, of course, hearing my parents talk about it in passing, but it wasn't until I got here that I realized just how true it was. Where I had cheat days, and a lot of them at that. They only allowed themselves one cheat meal a week. They weren't even peer pressured by their friends, who were all drinking, smoking, and doing other things at this party. In fact, their friends hadn't even offered me anything since they knew I was with them. It was a level of respect I hadn't seen in kids our age, but I liked it.

"She's cute." I nodded my head in the direction of a cute Indian girl across the room.

"That's Anushka. She's beautiful, but it'll never happen."

"Why not?" I frowned, looking over at Jagger.

He was the oldest of the Cruz brothers and I used to think he was the cutest until Mitchell bloomed. Also until I started spending every waking moment with him this summer. And kissed him. And did more than kiss him.

"Her parents have an arranged marriage set up for her."

"No way." My eyes widened. "People still do that?"

"Her parents did." He shrugged. "He's a cool dude, too. He picks her up from school on Fridays in his Porsche. He's probably somewhere . . . ." Jag stopped talking and looked around, finally stopping and pointing. "There."

I looked at the guy in question and blinked. "He's stupid handsome."

"So I hear." Jag chuckled.

"Damn, but really. I guess I wouldn't be opposed if my parents set me up with him."

"Thankfully Anu agrees."

"Wouldn't that be so weird?" I looked at him.

"Wouldn't what be weird?" Mitch asked, stopping in front of us, green eyes on me. My heart flipped.

"If our parents set us up in arranged marriages."

"You mean you and Jag?" Mitch frowned.

"I mean in general, but yeah, that would be a possibility." I shrugged.

"Hey, I'd be one helluva catch." Jag grinned.

"I'd probably have to kill you though," Mitch said. "And that would suck since I love you so much."

My pulse quickened. I felt myself redden. We hadn't told anyone about us. Not a soul. This felt like he was coming out with it and admitting it though, and I couldn't deny that it felt right. Jagger looked between the two of us and shook his head.

"I knew it."

"Knew what?" I laughed.

"I knew you two were up to something."

"What? How'd you know?" I asked, genuinely curious. We'd been so careful.

"Mitch won't let me go jogging with you in the morning. He doesn't invite me to the movies or bowling when you go."

"That's mean." I slapped Mitch on the arm and he caught my hand, pulling me into his chest.

"I can't help it if I want you all to myself."

"Okay. That's my cue. I'm going to be right over there," Jag said, walking away.

"I thought we weren't going to tell anyone." I looked up at him, head swimming with love and lust.

"Jag won't tell anyone."

"Your entire school is here. It's going to be difficult for you to get a girlfriend once I leave."

"So?" He shrugged a shoulder. "I've never been the boyfriend type anyway."

"Please." I sucked my teeth. "You've had girlfriends."

"Nope. You're my first one." He leaned down and kissed me with a reverence that quieted my jealousy, hesitation, and any questions I thought I had.

Chapter Twenty-Two

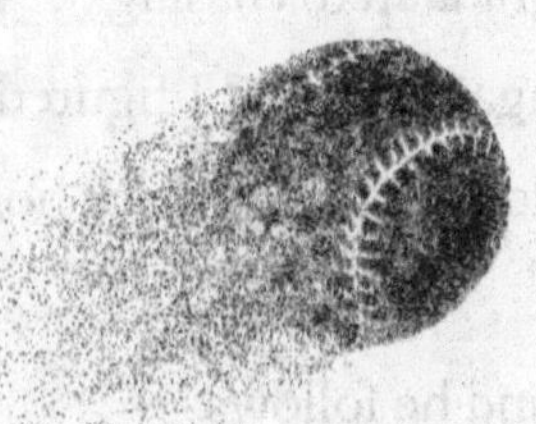

Present

"THANK YOU SO, SO MUCH FOR THE RIDE, KI. I OWE YOU one."

"It's no problem. I'm staying at my dad's tonight and he lives out here anyway."

"Really?" I glance over. "Where?"

"Right by the school."

"Don't tell me your dad works at UNC and you go to Duke." I laugh.

"Ummm . . . yeah." He laughs along. "In my defense, my mom went to Duke."

"Well, both my parents are UNC graduates." I grin.

"No fucking way."

"Yep."

"Damn." He laughs louder. "That's pretty savage. Do they still invite you over for Christmas?"

"They wish they didn't have to, but yeah."

"What in the world made you go to Duke? Defiance?"

"Something like that. My sister went to UNC. She's the good girl, the one who does everything right. I went to NYU when I first graduated, chasing . . . a stupid dream. My parents were so against it that I figured they wouldn't care where I went as long as I came back home."

"Do they care?"

"Yeah." I laugh, and he follows.

"My dad has tenure. History, but he specializes in African Studies. Every time we get together for a family reunion he gets made fun of by everyone. Most of my family pulls for UNC, they were around when MJ was there, you know? So they're die-hard."

"Ah, I get it. My mom's a dean."

"Damn, you really messed up." He chuckles as he parks in front of the building. "This you?"

"Yep." I point.

"What floor are you?"

"Ten."

"How many floors are there?" he leans forward and looks out the front window.

"Fourteen? I think fourteen."

"You think?" he laughs. "You don't pay attention in the elevator?"

"I mean, I will today." I unsnap my seat belt and pick up my purse from the floor before looking at him.

"We should hang out."

"We should."

"Maybe go on a date or something."

"Yeah, that would be fun."

"If this had been a date, I would kiss you right now."

"Next time then." I smile and open the door.

"Misty," he calls out as I get out of the car and shut the door. He lowers the window. "Next time."

"Thanks for the ride," I say with a wave and walk inside.

I'm still a little tipsy from the seltzers. I take my phone out and text Soleil to let her know I'm home and ask her if she's staying over at Archer's. My phone buzzes while the elevator is still on the tenth floor.

Soleil: I'm staying. Glad you're safe. Kian is cute.

I start typing and delete it. Kian is cute but he doesn't do it for me. I sigh, putting away my phone when the elevator chimes and opens in front of me. I feel the color drain from my face when my eyes clash with Mitchell, who's with the blonde from the party. I tear my gaze from his and push myself to walk past them, stepping into the elevator the moment they're no longer in it. I push the number ten three consecutive times, hoping no one else joins me in it. It shuts and then I'm moving and breathing a little easier when the distance is put between myself and Mitchell.

Chapter Twenty-Three

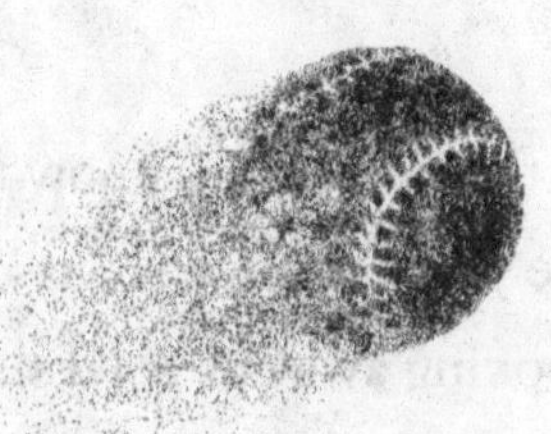

Past

MY SMILE WAS WIDE AS I OPENED THE DOOR FOR MITCHELL, but it fell the moment I saw the look on his face.

"What's wrong?" I opened the door wider and let him walk inside my aunt's apartment.

"We need to talk." He ran his fingers through his hair and dropped his hand with a slap against his waist.

"Okay." I shut the door quietly and walked over to him, heart tight in my chest because I already knew what he might say and I truly didn't want to hear it. "What's going on?"

"It's just . . ." He exhales and faces me, his green eyes sad as they hold my gaze. "We can't do this anymore."

"What do you mean?" I swallowed, feeling unshed tears build in my eyes. I took a step forward. He backed up.

"This. We can't be together. You're leaving tomorrow and this isn't going to work."

"Why not?" I frowned. "We're seeing each other on Thanksgiving. That's only a few months away. We can probably see each other for Labor—"

"No." His voice held a finality I hadn't heard before. "We had fun this summer. I'll always remember it, but it's over, Misty."

"But." I blinked, the unshed tears now trickling down my cheeks. "But I love you."

He grimaced, looking away as if I'd slapped him. As if what he was saying wasn't making my entire world feel like it was crumbling beneath my feet. I was the one who should've felt slapped, attacked, completely blindsided. He knew I loved him. We hadn't said it, but the way he looked at me, the way he touched me, I knew he loved me. He had to.

"You love me too," I said, voice gravelly and uneven. "I know you do."

"It doesn't matter." He met my gaze again and I could tell he was hurting. "Baseball is my number one love and I can't afford any distractions."

"So that's what I am now?" I swallowed the lump in my throat. "A distraction?"

"It was fun. It was great. I'll always cherish—"

"I don't give a fuck that you'll cherish it." I blinked more rapidly, hoping it would help clear my vision, but it didn't.

I could barely see him now. Maybe it was better that way. "Get out. Get out of my life."

I pointed toward the door. He stood there, unmoving, but only for a moment, then he left and shut the door behind him. I didn't know it was possible to physically feel a heart break, but I did. The pain in my chest was unbearable. I let my knees crash onto the carpet beneath me and continued to sob.

Chapter Twenty-Four

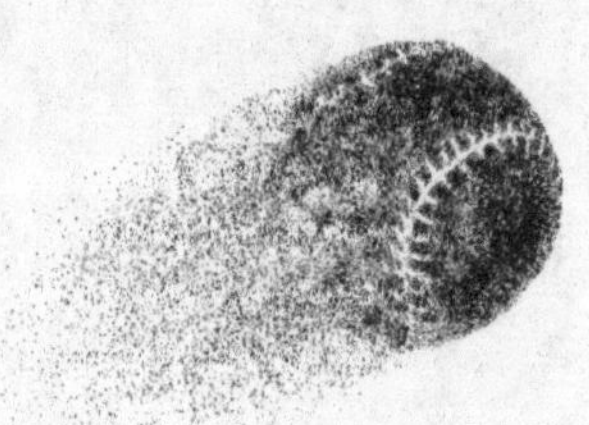

Present

'M STANDING ON THE SMALL BALCONY THAT OVERLOOKS THE quiet street when I hear my doorbell. Frowning, I click the vape in my hand to turn it off as I walk inside. When I look through the peephole, I don't expect to see Mitchell standing on the other side. Dylan, maybe. Not Mitchell. Definitely not Mitchell in a black T-shirt and gray lounge pants. I open the door slightly.

"What are you doing here?"

"I can't sleep." He runs his fingers through his dark hair with an exhale. "I've tried, Misty. I've tried to forget you and move on. I've tried to convince myself that you were a summer romance or just a friend, but then I see you at parties flirting with other guys or at family gatherings on the other side of the room trying to avoid me and I just can't do it anymore."

Because I'm essentially high, it takes me what feels like a full minute to process what he's saying, and even after I think I've processed it, I don't quite believe it. I tilt my head slightly and narrow my eyes up at him.

"I'm confused."

"About what?" He's looking at me like I've grown a second head. "I just . . . I thought that was very clear."

"Yeah, but . . . " I bring my vape up and shake it around. "I'm kinda high."

"I thought you stopped doing that."

"Well, I did, and then my anxiety laughed at me and I picked it back up again."

"So you don't understand me?" He frowns.

"Of course I understand you. I just don't understand why you're saying this to me at three o'clock in the morning. I don't understand why you're saying this to me after you've already brought a girl back to your apartment. I don't understand why you're saying this to me five years after we did what we did and you dismissed my feelings for you like they were nothing. So yeah, I'm confused."

"Oh." He drops his head. "I don't know. I don't know."

"Well, when you figure it out, come back and let me know because I'm not playing this game with you anymore. I'm not going to be your booty call or your side chick, or the girl you're on and off again with." I start closing the door, but his palm comes up to stop it. My eyes meet his and the determination in them makes my heart skip a beat.

"You were never a booty call or a side chick and would never be an off-and-on girl to me."

"I don't know what you want me to say to that," I whisper.

"Say you'll give me another chance."

I shake my head. "I can't."

"Please."

"I'm not looking for a relationship."

"That's fine. I'm fine with that."

"So, what, you want to hook up with me?" I let out a laugh. "Is that what it'll take for you to see we're not meant to be together?"

"Maybe." His eyes flash, a hint of lust.

"I'm willing to test that out if you are, but I'm telling you right now, you're going to get your heart broken." I raise an eyebrow, hoping I sound nonchalant when I feel anything but. I'm also hoping he doesn't call my bluff. Maybe he'll leave, maybe he'll—

He pushes the door open wider and walks in, two long steps forward that make me take three long steps back. His gaze is set on mine, unyielding, and when he reaches me and brings a hand up to cup my face, I don't move. His thumb caresses over my neck. I swallow, goosebumps spreading through me like wildfire. Bringing his face down, he kisses my lips. I feel myself sigh against him, my lips parting, my tongue ready to dance, explore, ready to let him do whatever it is he wants to me. I wish I wasn't so pliant. I wish I was pushing him away or acting like this isn't what I want, but that would be a lie because it's all a lie. Every single thing I said was. It's not his heart that'll break, it's mine. Again. For this, though? For this crackle and the fire that bubbles inside of me at his touch, I'll take that risk.

We kiss like we're trying to rip each other apart, like it's a competition of who will get there first. I push into the kiss hard and he walks me back until my knees hit the couch and we're both spilling over it, my back onto the cushions. I brace myself for his landing over me, but he breaks the kiss to catch himself and grabs my knee, opening my legs for him to step into. As soon as he does, I feel him, big and hard and ready for me. I meet his eyes again. This time, his hand cups me between my legs and his fingers begin to move against my mound. Sweet torture. My back bows off the couch, pleading for more. He delivers, sliding my shorts and panties to the side as his fingers slide into me, deep.

"You're so wet." He hisses, knuckle deep now, I'm pretty sure, since my eyes are rolling back and I feel him everywhere. "So wet."

"God. Please." I shut my eyes, panting, my hips moving against him.

I need this release. I need it. I need it. I need it. When I come, it's fireworks underneath my eyelids and through my body, an explosion of pent-up energy and a release that's years overdue. Not that I haven't had sex since we broke up. That's a lie. I've been with faceless men and we did bullshit things. When I open my eyes, Mitchell is looking down at me with an expression of complete wonder on his face. My heart skips again, and pulse racing, I grab him over his pants. He leans down over me, kissing me again, his lips bruising mine as I move my hand up and down, his low growl into my mouth pushing me to move my hand faster. He pulls away from the kiss and steps back slightly, my hand dropping onto my lap. He undresses and comes back to undress me completely, our clothes thrown in a heap across the room, the moonlight illuminating our naked bodies as he moves back and slides inside of me ever so slowly. I gasp at the feel of his girth, his length, his mouth on the side of my jaw when he bites me as he thrusts to the hilt.

We move together, his cock hitting a magical place inside of me that no one with the exception of my vibrator ever reaches, since no one else has cared to make the time to find it. Eyes on mine, he licks his thumb and brings it between us, sliding over my clit as he continues to move inside me, punishing thrusts that have my eyes rolling to the back of my head. Inside, I feel like I'm going to explode, like one more flick and my entire body will combust. My eyes pop open when I feel him pull out of me. His fingers move faster against my clit, his other hand pumping his cock as he watches me, and I start to come again as he comes on my stomach. It's a beautiful sight, watching Mitch come undone like that, but I remind myself that it's a short-lived moment of satisfaction because he won't be here tomorrow.

Chapter Twenty-Five

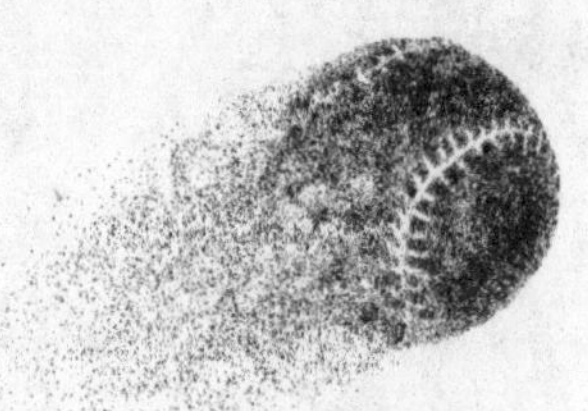

I GLANCE OVER AT THE EMPTY SPOT IN THE BED BESIDE ME AND sigh. What did I expect? For him to stay? I shake my head at myself and stretch my arms over my head as I yawn, then let them fall when I hear a noise. Sitting up quickly, I grab the sheet and cover myself when I hear footsteps approach my room. The door pushes open and Mitch smiles as he leans against the doorframe, a cup of coffee in his hand.

"Hey."

I blink. "Hey."

"I brought you this and a bagel. Cream cheese on the side." He winks, pushes off the doorframe, and walks over to me, setting the coffee beside me on the nightstand. He kisses the top of my head and walks back out of the room like this is normal.

I take a sip of coffee, then get out of bed and rush to the bathroom. Once I'm done getting ready, I walk back out into the living room and find Mitch, foot propped on the coffee table, watching ESPN, eating a donut. He looks over and checks me out, his gaze like a caress over every inch of my body, the way his fingers were multiple times last night. I fight a blush.

"I thought you brought bagels?"

"I did." He stands up, taking the last bite of his donut, and walks over to me. He kisses my mouth, a long, chaste kiss that leaves me dumbfounded. What is even happening? "You don't like donuts though."

"I don't." I frown. "How do you know all of these random things about me?"

"I pay attention. When we went to Colorado that year, everyone got Krispy Kreme and you said you only liked the hot chocolate."

"That was like three years ago." My frown deepens as I walk over to the bag where I assume the bagels are. "You're so weird."

"Because I pay attention?" He chuckles.

"Yeah, that's some real stalker shit." I pull out an everything bagel and slather light cream cheese, a quarter of what they spread on bagels in places.

"Yeah, well, I guess I'm a stalker then."

I take a bite and look up at him. He's standing on the other side of the counter staring at me. "What?"

"Nothing." He smiles. "Last night was . . ."

"Good. Yeah, I agree." I swallow. "It's not happening again."

"Right." He laughs.

"I'm serious."

"Famous last words." He shoots me a look. "We both know it's happening."

"What exactly do you want?" I set the bagel down. "A booty call?"

"No. We went over this. No. I want you."

"You want me." I scoff. "Is baseball still your first love?"

"I mean . . . " He reaches a hand and cups the back of his neck, looking away briefly. "I love it, yeah."

"Is it the number one thing in your life?"

"Yes."

"Then no." I shrug.

"No." He walks around the counter. "No. I mean, yes it is but only because I don't have you."

"Me?" I laugh, putting a hand up. "Mitchell. Please."

"I'm not kidding." He stands flush against me, bringing an arm around my waist. Begrudgingly, I tilt my neck and meet his eyes. "I'm not kidding, Misty. I don't want it. If I don't have you by my side, what's the point? I fucked up. We were young and I was stupid and blinded by ambition."

"And now?"

"And now I'm no longer blinded by it."

"Sure." I roll my eyes. "Mister let's get up at five thirty in the morning for a run before I kill myself in the gym room and then on the mound practicing my closing pitches?"

"I'm serious." He lets go of me and puts some distance between us. "I thought I was going straight to the majors after high school. I mean, Dad did it." He shrugs. "And then I got hurt."

"I didn't even know you got hurt. I mean, I heard about it, but I didn't realize what that meant."

"I was out half the season because of my injury and landed in the thirtieth round of the draft, so I opted for college instead."

"Why?" I frown.

"I knew, everyone knew, I deserved to be in the first round."

"So you decided to come here instead of the minors?"

"I figured I'd come here, heal, practice, get better, and then see what they offered."

"I'm still waiting for the part where you explain how it's not your first love or how you're no longer blinded by ambition."

"I love baseball. It's in my blood. You know." He shrugs a shoulder. I nod, because I do know. Most Dominicans live and breathe baseball from the moment we're born, whether we play the sport or not. "My brothers took the easy route. They picked other sports so they wouldn't have to live in Dad's shadow, and it's a fucking big shadow. My entire life I've been compared to him, people whisper about me never reaching his grandeur."

"You can't let other people's opinions define you." I place a hand on his chest.

"You said that to me once. Remember?" He brings his forehead to mine. "I miss you, Misty. I miss having you on my side."

"I've always been on your side," I whisper. "I don't have to be with you to be on your side."

"I want you to be with me and be on my side," he whispers back. "I'm tired of waiting in the bullpen."

"You put yourself in the bullpen. You were it for me. In my eyes, you were the starting pitcher and you ruined that."

"Because I was scared."

"Yeah, well, I can't afford getting my heart broken because you're scared." I pull away. "I just can't. I have enough crap on my plate to fill it with yours."

"I promise you won't regret it."

"What do you want, Mitchell?" I cross my arms.

"I want you to be my girlfriend."

"Why would you even want a girlfriend? I saw all those girls all over you last night."

"I don't want any of them."

"Not even the blonde?" I shoot him a look.

"Especially not the blonde." His lips twitch. "I didn't do anything with her. She used our bathroom and then I walked her downstairs to make sure she'd leave."

"Right." I roll my eyes. "The good ol' bathroom excuse."

"She used it." He chuckles. "It didn't work. How could it? I was watching you all night. I wanted to kill that guy you left with. I wanted to grab you and take you to a corner and pull up that miniskirt you had on and fuck you right there in front of everyone."

"That would've been quite the show." I feel my face burn up.

He fills the distance between us, wrapping an arm around me and pulling me against him once more. "Be my girlfriend."

"I really don't want a boyfriend."

"Why not?"

I bite my lip. *Because you ruined that for me. Because I refuse to let someone hurt me the way you did, especially you.* I sigh, not saying any of that. It wouldn't be fair or make sense. We're both different people now and I know that.

"I think we're better off as friends." I look up at him.

"I disagree."

"So I've heard." I roll my eyes. "You disagree with this every time I say it."

"Let me take you out on a date then. At least give me that."

I sigh. "What's the point, Mitch?"

"I don't know." He shrugs. "Maybe I'll manage to convince you we're good together."

"Doubtful." I frown.

The doorbell rings and three loud knocks follow.

"I have practice." Mitch pulls back with a sigh.

"Yo, hurry up," one of them screams from the other side of the door. Dylan, I think.

"I guess you should go." I lean against the counter.

"So, yes on the date thing?" he asks. "I'm going to take it as a yes."

"I have to think about it."

"Misty." He groans. "Come on."

Another loud pound on the door. "Mitch, bro, we're leaving."

"I have to go."

"Go."

"Just say yes." He flashes me one of those panty-dropping grins of his that I'm sure works on every person on the planet.

"I'll think about it." I walk toward the door and open it, looking outside. "Hey, guys."

"Sell out," Mitch says, brushing past me and walking outside.

"Have fun at practice," I sing-song as I shut the door and lock it.

I take a deep breath and let it out before getting my ass into gear. I have a shift in like twenty minutes and I want to try to leave early so I can go hang out with my sister at my parents' house later.

Chapter Twenty-Six

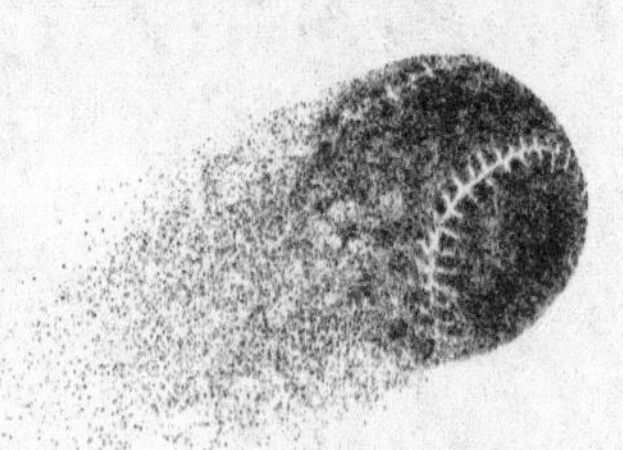

Mitch

"**C**OME ON, CRUZ. POINT YOUR FUCKING GODDAMN FOOT," Coach Wallace yells.

"I am!" I let my arms hit my sides with an exhale.

I've been working on my speed all fucking morning and I'm just not feeling it today. My father would call my bluff and tell me it's bullshit. He'd say that I have to make myself feel it even when I think I don't. He'd also tell me to get rid of all distractions in order to ensure my ninety-four mile an hour fastball. It's the reason he's great. He's able to fully separate his personal life from his career. When he played professionally, he was able to forget fights with Mom or issues with us and go out there and kill it every single time he had a game. I'm not him though. I would love to say I'm better than him, but that would be a total fucking lie. By my age, he'd been in the Show for three years already. He'd been recruited while he was still living in the Dominican Republic and set up in training camp when he was barely a teenager.

We've had a completely different life. A completely different upbringing, and yet, the comparison will always be there. Everyone, from scouts to coaches to journalists on ESPN, forgets about all of that when they compare us. They see numbers and stats. As they should. I set up for another pitch and focus on my movements. It's this motion that got me from eighty-nine to ninety-two when I was a senior in high school. My goal has been ninety-four for a while now and even though I can throw it, it's not consistent enough for my liking. Or my coach's, for that matter. So I try again. I stop thinking about Misty and the possibility that's so close yet so far. I stop thinking about the scouts who are watching me like hawks. I stop thinking about the draft I'm going to enter after this season is over. I stop wondering if they're going to pay me more than they originally offered and if I made a grave mistake by not taking it at the time. I just stop. If this was a game, it would be easier. During games, it's easy for me to shut it all out. When it's just me and Coach Wallace it's a little different. Maybe it's the noise I need. Maybe it's the smell of sweat, beers, and hot dogs. Maybe it's the cheers or the boos or the pressure of closing a perfect game. Whatever it is, it doesn't exist in this moment, but I pretend. I make myself believe all of those things are happening as I set up this mechanic that's become second nature to me already.

"Ninety-three," Coach Wallace says. "You got this, kid."

I do another one. And another one. And another one.

Ninety-three each time.

"Fuck." I take a breath.

"We're out of time. I don't want you overthrowing if you're so dead set on pitching tonight," he says. "You'll get there."

"Yeah." I pick up the ball and toss it into the bucket beside me.

"Are your parents coming tonight?"

"I don't know. They'll definitely be there this weekend though." I pick up my bag, hoist it over my shoulder, and say goodbye.

As I walk out, I take it all in. This is one of my last practices here. These are my last three regular season games before we go to Charlotte for the ACC championship next weekend. It's scary and exciting and I realize that maybe that's one of the reasons I'm dying for Misty to give me a chance so badly. She's already the one who got away and a part of me feels like maybe if I get her now I can secure her forever. My brother Mav would tell me it's a stupid way to think, let alone talk, about a woman. Jagger would tell me I'm being a simp. I wouldn't disagree with either of them in this particular instance, but I also don't want to hear it, so I'm not going to tell them about any of it.

Chapter Twenty-Seven

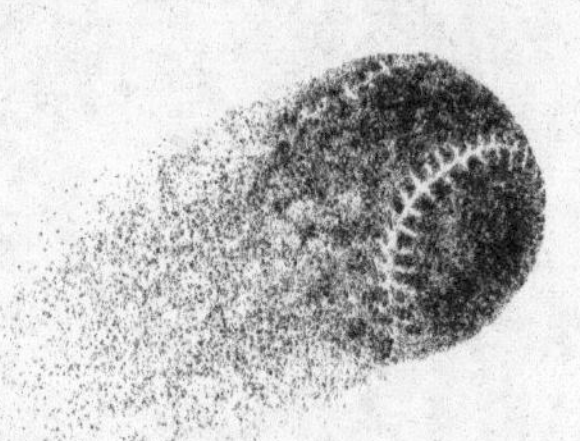

Misty

"**Y**OU DID NOT TELL ME WE WERE GOING TO THE GAME." I glare at my sister.

"I thought you were going for sure. You're writing a damn article on them."

"Yes, but I wasn't planning on going to tonight's game. I was planning on hanging out with you."

"Well, Jag got us tickets, so we're going, and you're coming with."

"I don't even have a ticket."

"Misty, please." She shoots me a look. "It's like you don't know who our parents are. Or theirs."

"This is going to be so awkward," I mutter under my breath as she walks inside and I follow.

"Hi, Mom. Dad. Jag." I kiss each of them on the cheek. They're all wearing baby blue shirts, ready to go support their baby blue team. Normally, I truly do not care about the rivalry. Truly. But when it comes to this, it bothers me.

"I'll be right back." I run up the stairs to my old room and pull out a Duke T-shirt. It's a basketball shirt, but it doesn't matter. A sport is a sport. When I run back down, the four of them laugh hysterically.

"You're really going to sit behind home plate wearing that?" Mom asks.

"Yes." I roll my eyes. "It's not like the people playing don't know what school I go to and everyone else can kiss my ass."

"Misty!" Mom says.

"Fine. My butt."

"Let's go." Dad shakes his head. "I hate getting there late."

"You only like getting there early so you can have a beer and a hot dog before the game and then again during the fourth inning."

"When was the last time we went to a game together?" Dad asks, raising an eyebrow. "But alas, you're right."

"Is Mavy coming?" I ask when we get outside. "I haven't heard from him."

"Yeah, he'll meet us there. Rocky had practice today, so he's waiting for her."

"So things are getting serious."

"I'd say." Jagger nods.

"Good for him. Rocky is such a great girl," Mom says. "And her parents are such good people."

I smile and nod in agreement. They really are. "And Ms. Bev makes amazing beef patties."

"I'd kill for a pattie with coco bread," Dad says as we get in the car.

"Me too." My stomach growls. I put a hand over it. "I had a croissant an hour ago, but I'm starving."

"That's because you don't eat," Mom says.

"Here we go." I roll my eyes.

"You don't."

"Okay, Mom." I sigh. "I'll get a hot dog and beer before the first inning starts."

"Oh my God." Mom shakes her head. "You better not get drunk at this game."

"With one beer?" I laugh. "Please, Mom. I'm Dominican, show some respect."

They laugh and I keep smiling.

"So, how's following Mitchell around? Is he being a pain in the ass?" Jag asks.

"When is he not?" I look out the window in hopes to hide my blush. My sister nudges me hard. I shoot her a look.

"I know that face."

"It's nothing." I smile.

"Bullshit," she whispers.

"We'll talk about it later."

Thankfully, she drops it, and Dad starts talking to Jagger about shoulders, which means the rest of us stay quiet the rest of the ride over.

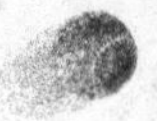

I was lying when I said I didn't get drunk off one beer. I had one, fast, on an empty stomach, and I definitely feel a little lightheaded. I say this to my sister, who laughs and hooks her arm around mine.

"You're such a clown, Mist."

"I know." I yawn.

"So, Mitch?"

"Mitch is Mitch." I shrug. "He wants me to be his girl-friend. I turned him down."

"And that's it?"

"Yes."

"Bullshit. He asks you out every time he sees you and you turn him down every time. Normally, you act all pissed off at the sound of his name alone. What's changed?"

"I hate you." I give her a side-eye. "But we had sex."

"What? When?"

"Last night. He showed up after that party I told you about and it just sort of happened."

"Sort of happened? Why'd you cave?" She pushes my shoulder with hers when I don't immediately answer. "Misty."

"I don't know. He was at that party heavily flirting with me and then he showed up and he looked so good and said all the right things."

"But you still don't want to be in a relationship with him."

"Hell no."

"Why not? You know he'd treat you like a queen if he got another chance."

"I don't care."

"Yes you do." She lets go of my arm so we can walk down to the seats, which are in the first row, right behind home plate.

We sit—my mom, me, Josephine, Jagger, my dad, Maverick, Rocky, and a friend of hers. The game starts, I'm half paying attention, but mostly talking to my mother and sister about her wedding, which she's planning for August.

"I really, really do not like purple," I say. "It's just so played out, and it's summer. Do something different."

"Like what? I don't want orange or yellow."

"Pink. Mint green! That's different."

"Mint green?" Mom pulls a face. "No, honey. This is not the eighties."

"All colors are for all decades, Mom." I shoot her a look.

"But not purple." She shoots me a look right back.

"Purple doesn't look good on me," I say finally.

Jo laughs. "I knew this was about you."

"Well, you'll be wearing white. Who else would this be about?" I ask, then shout, "Jag, what color do you like for the wedding?"

"Oh no." He shakes his head. "I am not getting involved. I'll be at the altar, but that's it."

"Oh, come on, at least say you hate purple for the bridesmaids."

"I hate purple," he says, then winks at my sister.

"Okay, no purple."

"I seriously think pink, like a light coral-ish pink would look bomb," I say.

"Or evergreen," Rocky shouts from the other side.

"Evergreen," I say excitedly. "That looks good on my skin tone."

"Mine too," Rocky says with a laugh.

"See? Listen to the brown girls."

"Pink would look nice," Mom says.

"Thank you." I look at my sister.

"Come to Charlotte next weekend. We'll go dress shopping."

"Cool. We can also have your bachelorette if everyone will be there."

"Oh no. We want a joint bachelor slash bachelorette," Jo says. "Right, babe?"

"I'm down for whatever. Let's go somewhere though. Vegas?" he asks.

"I'm down for Vegas, but it's played out," I say.

"You think everything is played out."

"Because it freaking is. Everyone does everything everyone else does. It's annoying, but I do understand why Vegas is on the to-do list for this." I sigh.

"If we keep it small, we can go anywhere," Jagger says.

"Let's go, Tar Heels," Dad screams. "Let's go, baby!"

We all look back at the field. There are two outs, a man on second, and one up to bat currently.

"That's Dylan," I shout. "Go, Dylan!"

"While she's wearing a fucking Duke shirt," my sister says, shaking her head.

"So embarrassing," Mom says.

My jaw drops. "You guys are embarrassing. What the heck?"

"And she's demanding she picks the colors for our wedding," Jagger says. "Maybe we should just go with Carolina blue."

"Oh, fuck no." I glare at my sister, who is laughing. "Don't you dare, Josephine."

"But I love Carolina blue," Jo says innocently.

"I will riot."

"It's her wedding, love."

I hear the bat make contact with the ball and look at the game just in time to see it leave the park. We all stand up, cheering loudly.

"When does Mitch play?" Jo asks.

I shrug a shoulder.

"Now." Jag chuckles, glancing over at me. "You really haven't been to a game, huh?"

"No, I've been to practices though. I usually work when they have games, or have prior commitments." I smile. Honestly, I haven't wanted to go to a game by myself and Soleil actually works nights, and I don't want to bring Archer, so yeah, I've been avoiding this.

"Welp, they just struck out so I guess we'll get to see our boy play now," Mom says.

Our boy. Jesus Christ on a cracker. She makes it worse by pulling out her phone and hitting record. She doesn't record the field though, she stands up and records the stands. I'm about to tell her she looks ridiculous, but the crowd starts going wild. Wild, wild. Screaming louder than I've ever heard at any baseball game that's not a World Series. I look around, confused, then look at my sister, who's laughing at the expression on my face.

"What is happening?" I'm still looking around, for a mascot throwing free T-shirts or something, when my sister grabs my face and points it at the field.

Mitchell is jogging to the mound, waving his glove with a huge grin on his face as everyone continues to go completely bananas.

"This is for Mitch?" I shout, still confused.

"Dude, he's a fucking god," Jagger says. "You've been missing out."

The way he says it, I don't know if he's talking about me not seeing his brother playing or about not hooking up with his brother, so I choose not to respond just in case. Instead, I look back onto the field, where Mitch is setting up, pushing his shoulders back and bending his elbows as his eyes zone in on the glove he's targeting. I know he's looking at the glove and not at me, but my body didn't get the memo and my heart starts pounding harder, faster. He strikes the first guy out, and the crowd goes wild again. It's a mixture of Tar Heels and *theeeeeeeeee troublemaker*, which seriously makes me laugh, because how corny is that? I say this to my sister, who shrugs like she sort of likes it.

"It's because he gives everyone trouble," Dad mansplains.

"Gee, I had no idea it could have meant that," I say.

"Be nice, Misty." That's Mom, under her breath, since she's still recording.

He strikes the second guy out.

"That's right, baby." Jagger and Maverick stand up, clapping.

When the third strike out comes, everyone goes wild again.

"I hope you're taking notes, suckers," Mav says.

I laugh loudly. Mitch is the first batter up this time. He makes contact with the ball, but the pitcher catches it and he runs back to the bullpen. As he does, he glances over and winks, and I swear if I wasn't bright red already this is the moment I would be. That is, until some girl behind me says, "Oh my gosh that was totally to you. He was totally looking at you."

I glance over my shoulder with a scowl and look at the two of them. They're doing a much better job than I am at being Mitchell's number one fan. They're both wearing sky blue cropped shirts that say CRUZ 8 on the front. Obviously homemade, which makes it even cuter. I turn back around and face the field again.

Jo nudges me. "He was winking at you."

"Well, they think it was at them and that's okay. They're actually here to see him."

"And you're not?" She raises an eyebrow.

I dip down into my seat and cross my arms. The cheering for Mitchell does not subside in the least and I realize that if this is how it is at a collegiate level, I'll never have him to myself. Not really anyway. Though, Jagger plays professional football and he's obsessed with my sister and acts like he has separation anxiety when the Panthers go out of town, so maybe Mitch would be similar. Not that I want him to be super dependent on me, but it would be nice not to have to worry about him cheating. I groan. The girlfriend of an athlete life is just not for me.

Chapter Twenty-Eight

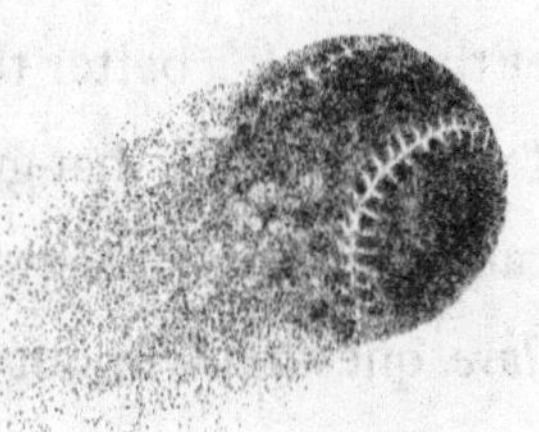

Mitch

S HE'S ONLY LOOKED IN MY DIRECTION ONCE SINCE WE GOT TO her parents' house and it's killing me. I play it cool though, talking to my brothers, her parents, her sister, basically everyone but her. It's what I've been doing for five years, what both of us have been doing. We ignore each other and when we do end up talking just the two of us it always ends up in a bickering argument. Not this time though. If pushing aside all the things I really want to say to her is the only way to get her to be amicable and agree to go out with me, then so be it. In the past she's called me pushy and claimed I want her to be with me and only me while I'm out playing the field. She has a right to that claim, of course. Not that I've ever brought a girl to any of our family gatherings, but still, people talk and I know she's heard a thing or two about my sexcapades.

I guess the reason it bothers me is that she's not a saint either, which gives her no room to judge. Good for her for not sitting around waiting for the one perfect guy to come sweep her off her feet though. It's better that she's aware that he doesn't exist. I wish I could be that guy, but who the heck am I kidding? I can't even answer the straightforward, *is baseball still my first love*, question without messing it up. I hate that question. I hate it more when she's the one asking because I know whatever I say is tied up into it all.

"I can't believe you're going into the draft and you're only one year away from graduating," Misty's mom Rosa says, lamenting.

"He's an athlete," her dad says. "He needs to strike while he can."

"I understand that, Henry, but this child has a perfect GPA."

"You have a perfect GPA?" Misty asks, surprised. It's the first thing she's asked about me and even though no one bats an eye, it's a big deal to me.

"Four point oh, baby." I wink at her. She reddens instantly and I almost feel bad. Almost. Maybe I would if she didn't look so cute when she's embarrassed.

"Wow," she says. "Impressive."

"What's your major?" Jo asks. "I always forget."

"Finance."

"Finance." Jo's brows lift. "So if the baseball thing didn't work out, which, we all know it will, what would you do with your major?"

"Probably financial planning. I like the idea of helping people stay out of debt."

"That's nice," Misty says, smiling a little. "Maybe I should've gone into finance."

"I told you you'd regret journalism." Her mother shakes her head.

"*Déjala*, Rosa," Henry says, shushing his wife. "Misty also has impeccable grades."

"That doesn't surprise me." I smile at Misty, who tears her gaze away from me.

"What's your dream team?" Rocky asks. "Still Yankees?"

"Always."

"Always," Jagger echoes.

"Rocky's hoping you say Mets." Maverick throws an arm around Rocky. "I keep telling her not to hold her breath."

"I mean, if the Mets sign me, I'd be cool with it." I shrug and laugh at the look everyone except Rocky is giving me.

Everyone pulls for the team their parents root for. It's human nature. For us, it's a little more personal, since Dad played for the Yankees. Henry had been recruited and signed by them as well before an injury forced him out of the league. In hindsight, it was probably the best thing that happened to him since he became a successful doctor, but I can't imagine it was easy to come to terms with it. We continue our conversation about baseball and pitchers and teams that may be interested in me, and I watch Misty to try to gauge a reaction, but find none. I wish she was a little easier to read, the way she was that summer, before she started guarding her emotions and words from me. I know I fucked up, but I don't think we're past the point of no return.

We can't be. She has to give me one more chance.

Chapter Twenty-Nine

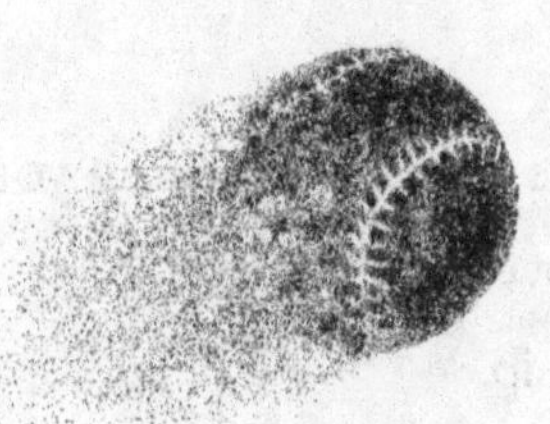

Misty

'M BONE TIRED WHEN I HEAR THE DOORBELL THE NEXT MORNING, but I get up, brush my teeth, and open it anyway. Mitchell is standing there looking bright-eyed, with a smile on his face that I would probably swoon over if I wasn't so exhausted.

"You're making coffee." I put a hand up and turn around, heading back to my room to change.

I'm fast today, and when I open the door to my room, I inhale the scent of freshly brewed coffee, and I feel like I just might be ready for our jog after all.

"I hope it's okay. No sugar, two creams?" He slides a mug to my side of the counter.

"Perfect." I take a sip. I take it with one cream, but how can I complain?

"You made me feel like a traitor last night." He sets his elbows on the counter and leans forward, eyes on mine.

"How?"

"Wearing that Duke shirt in the stands."

"Wouldn't I be the traitor? Not you?" I take another sip to hide my smile.

"Not when I was the one checking you out all night, wishing I could run over and kiss you."

"Hm." Another sip.

"Come on, Misty." He sighs, standing and running his fingers through his hair. "One date. At least one date. What are you so afraid of?"

"A lot of things." I set the mug down and stand straighter. "I just don't think it's a good idea. My sister and your brother are getting married. You hear of families being torn apart all the time when siblings end up together and then break up."

"That wouldn't happen." He frowns. "And I'm asking for one date, not your hand in marriage."

"Well, that's good because I would never marry you." I start walking toward the door. "Are we going on this stupid jog or what?"

"Jesus." He's on my heels as I open the door and walk to the elevator. "What the hell did I say wrong now?"

"Nothing." I punch the button and cross my arms,

looking straight ahead at our reflection in the steel. He's so much taller than I am. If I turn sideways to punch him right now it would land on his chest. I let out a breath and step inside once the doors open. Once inside, I push the lobby button and cross my arms again.

"Misty." He sighs.

"It's fine. Just drop it."

He does. We walk to the other side of the street and start to jog in silence. Amazingly, I don't feel like I'm going to pass out at any moment and complete the jog with him.

"You sure you don't want to do another round?" he asks, cool as a cucumber when we get back to our starting point.

"Positive."

"I think you can do it if you push."

"I have no interest."

"We keep doing half a mile." He chuckles. "You can totally do the whole thing now."

"Nope." I start walking toward the entrance of the park. "Knock yourself out though."

He doesn't say anything, but I hear him jogging over to me once I get far enough.

"You're impossible, you know?" he says when he reaches me.

"I've heard that once or twice."

"Do you want to grab breakfast?"

"No, thank you." I keep my voice casual, nice, grateful.

"Not even for your article?"

I let out a long breath. The damn article that I can't seem to write? The one I need to get done in order to graduate? The one his mother wants to publish in her magazine (if it's good)? I groan.

"You did start the article, right?" he asks as we're crossing the street.

"Yep." I have two sentences written, so that's a start.

"When is it due?"

"A week."

"One week?" he asks. "When can I read it?"

"When it's published." *If it's published.*

"Are you dedicating it to anyone?"

"Huh?" I frown, glancing at my watch momentarily as a message from my sister comes in. I ignore it and look at Mitchell. "What are you talking about?"

"The article. You know you can dedicate it to someone."

"Why in the world? It's not a book."

"It's still a body of work. You can dedicate your thesis to someone." He shrugs a shoulder and opens the door to the lobby for me. "Why not this?"

"I just don't see the point. Why are you asking, you want me to dedicate it to you?"

"No." He chuckles. "I was just curious."

My watch buzzes again as we get to the elevator. This time, when my sister asks if I want breakfast, I push the little button and voice back, "I work. You can come by the coffee shop though."

"So that's why you turned me down." Mitch shoots me an amused look as we get out of the elevator.

"I turned you down because I have no interest in going on a breakfast date with you."

"Dinner then."

I sigh. "I don't see the point, Mitch." I turn the key and open the door.

"I know you still have feelings for me."

"What?" I swallow, turning around to face him.

"Do you?" He searches my eyes.

"I don't know what you want me to say."

"The truth."

"I don't know why it matters."

"It just does."

"Even if I have feelings for you, it wouldn't change anything. I still wouldn't be tripping all over myself to be with you."

"Because I hurt you."

"Yeah. You know what they say about insanity."

"We were seventeen, Misty." He leans against the doorframe, peering down at me through those dark lashes of his. He reaches out and caresses the side of my arm, sending a shiver down my body. "Don't let fear get in the way of your dreams."

"My dreams?" I laugh. "I don't know what inspirational posters you've been reading, but I'm pretty sure this is your dream, not mine."

"What if it is?" He smiles and God, it does something to me.

"Pick me up tonight at seven. I have to be up early, so no later than that."

"Yes, ma'am." He beams as he stands up straight and salutes me, like I'm a superior he's following orders from.

"Goodbye, Mitchell." I step inside fully and shut the door between us, heart pounding.

As I shower and dress for work, I remind myself that I need to keep this casual, the way I do with everyone else. Just because he gives me goosebumps or butterflies doesn't mean he's it for me. Whatever I feel for him is a memory of what I felt before, but I can't get my hopes up. He's leaving soon and I have no idea where he'll end up but I know it wouldn't work out between us once he's gone.

Chapter Thirty

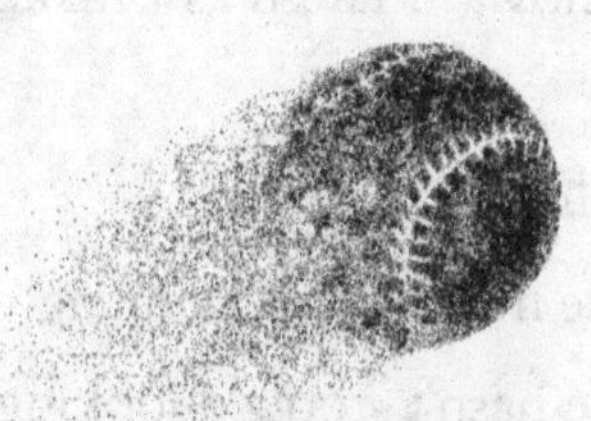

I'M HELPING ARCHER PUT AWAY A SHIPMENT OF FOOD AND DRINKS when my sister and Jagger walk through the door. Behind them, Mitchell walks in, head down as he types furiously into his phone.

"I got this," Archer says. "We only have a few more juices left to bring up front. You go take their order."

"Thanks." I wipe my hands on my apron and walk over to the register, but before I take their order, I walk around and give my sister and Jagger a quick hug. Luckily, Mitch is still on the phone so I ignore him.

"I forgot how cute this place is," Jo says, looking around. "I'm surprised it's this empty."

"It's early. Only early morning coffee drinkers have come in. Everyone else is either sleeping or at church."

I take their orders, Mitchell included once he puts down his phone and pays attention, and because it's so empty, I'm able to take their stuff to their table and talk to them a little longer. After a moment, I go back behind the counter and take a new customer's order.

"That's the ex," Archer says.

"How do you know?" I laugh as I make an oat milk cappuccino.

"The tension is rising."

"Shut up." I shake my head, still smiling.

"It's true. And he hasn't stopped looking at you since he got here."

"He's been on the phone the entire time since he got here." I shoot Archer a look as I froth the milk.

"So you've been looking at him the entire time then."

"Whatever." I roll my eyes.

"What happened with Kian?"

"He gave me a ride home."

"And?"

"He asked me out."

"And?"

"I said yes." I shrug a shoulder as I focus on pouring the milk into the coffee. I've been practicing making cute designs with the milk, but so far I've only been able to master a leaf.

"When are you going out?"

"I don't know." I finish preparing the drink, set the mug on a plate, and push it toward the edge of the counter.

"Probably never," Archer says, eyeing Mitch quickly. "I don't think he's letting you out of his sight any time soon."

"Please." I roll my eyes, then smile. "Soleil said she went home with you the other night."

"Ah, the swift subject change," he says, but his ears are bright red and he's smiling. "I think it's going somewhere."

"I knew it." I feel myself smile wide. "You guys are perfect for each other."

"Okay, Cupid. Pipe down." He laughs lightly and I can tell he's super embarrassed, so I stop talking about it. Archer glances over my shoulder and back at me. "Pissed-off customer in aisle one. I'm going to run to the bank to make this deposit. I'll be right back." He taps my head, grabs the stuff he needs, and walks toward the front door. I turn around to see a pissed-off Mitchell.

"What's up?" I walk over. "Did you not like your coffee?"

"It's fine."

"The croissant?"

"It's good."

"Okay so why are you mad?"

"I'm not mad. Can we talk?"

"Right now?"

"Yes."

"Okay, talk." I glance around.

There's no one else here besides my sister and Jagger and they're lost in conversation, probably still looking at wedding venues. Instead of spilling out whatever he's thinking from across the counter, Mitchell walks around and stands in front of the register.

"What are you doing?" I whisper, eyes wide.

"Talking."

"Okay." My heart pounds harder, faster against my chest. "What is it?"

"I hate seeing you with other guys."

"Archer?" I nearly squeal. "He's a friend."

"I know. I'm not saying I hate the fact that you have guy friends. I know he's a friend and he seems like a cool dude, but I hate it. I hate that you laugh with him and talk to him so carefree and with me you seem all wound up and guarded." He takes another step forward. "I hate that you feel like you can't be yourself around me and I hate that I know exactly how you are when you're yourself because you let me see you once, before I fucked it all up."

I lick my lips. "You did fuck it all up."

"Do you need me to apologize again?"

"No. You've apologized enough." He has, over the years, every time we see each other and we're left alone he apologizes and I'm tired of it. "We were kids and you were right."

"About what?" He frowns.

"About not having room in your life for more than one love. You were right to break it off. Now look at you."

"Mitch, we're going to head out," Jagger calls out. I glance over to see him and my sister standing and picking up the table.

"I'll do that." I brush past Mitch and walk over to them, taking what I can from Jagger's hands and then my sister. "I'm sorry we couldn't hang out today. I would've called out, but Arch needed someone to cover Austin's spot."

"Austin is the cute, nerdy guy?" Jo asks. "With the Pokémon card collection?"

"How do you know so much about this guy?" Jagger frowns.

"That's the one." I laugh. "He's at a convention this weekend."

"For Pokémon?" Jo blinks.

"Yep."

"This is the guy you're sort of dating?" she asks, as if I know a ton of Pokémon collectors.

"You're dating someone?" Mitchell asks. "When did this happen?"

"I'm not." I sigh and shoot my sister a look. "We're not dating."

"Last time we spoke about him you said you were going on a date."

"Yeah, but that was a while ago."

"Who is this guy?" Mitch asks. "The guy you took to the dinner?"

"Yes." I glance over at him.

"He does have a mean card collection," he tells Jagger.

"Does he have that rare Charizard?" Jag asks.

"I wouldn't be surprised."

"I'm sure Austin will be happy to know his collection is being discussed in such detail," I say, walking back over to the counter to drop off the things in my hands.

"Are you really dating him?" Mitch asks, walking over to me.

"I'm not dating anyone exclusively." I turn around and look at him. "I already told you that."

"Oh fuck. This is our cue," Jagger says, glancing at his watch. "If you want us to drop you off at the training facility, let's go, bro. We need to head home."

"I have to go." Mitch looks at me. "See you at seven."

I nod as my sister pulls me into a hug, and then say goodbye to Jag and Mitch again before going back to work.

Chapter Thirty-One

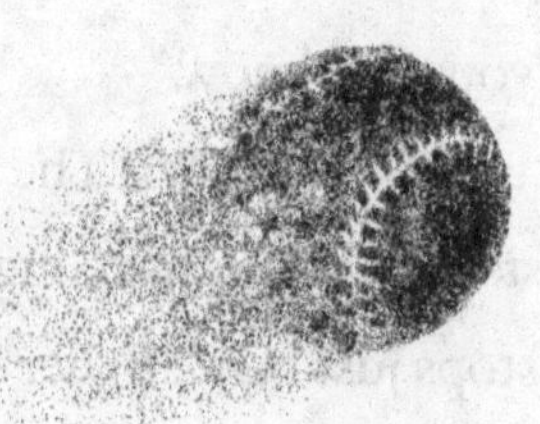

Mitch

DESPERATION. THAT'S WHAT I FEEL CRAWLING THROUGH ME as the day goes on. I tried to exhaust myself of it during practice, but it's no use. I cannot get her out of my head. At six thirty, I look in the mirror and take a deep breath. I got this. I walk out of my room and find that we have visitors. Normally, this doesn't bother me. We're allowed to bring anyone we want into our shared space, but Silvie is here with her friends and the last thing I need right now is to deal with her. Dylan looks at me and shakes his head, like he knows what I'm thinking and he's regretful about it. I ignore him and them, and instead of saying hello and being courteous as I normally would, I grab my keys and walk out the door. I'm ringing Misty's doorbell when the door to my apartment opens and shuts and Silvie shows up.

"You're not going to even say hi?" she asks, obviously upset.

"Hi." I look at the door in front of me again, hoping Silvie gets a clue and gets lost.

"I came here for you, you know."

"I didn't ask you to." I look at her. The door opens beside me and Misty is standing there wearing wide leg jeans and a black shirt that stops just beneath her breasts. It takes me a second to regain my thoughts and pick up my jaw from the ground.

"I thought you weren't the dating type," Silvie says. Misty peeks her head out of her apartment and glances over at Silvie, who looks at her.

"Silvie." I take a deep breath and exhale. "Please don't do this right now. Just go back to your friends or mine and let's call it a night."

"He's a fucking asshole," Silvie says to Misty.

"Oh, I know," Misty responds. "Which is why I don't understand why you're still chasing him. Move on."

"Don't tell me to move on." Silvia blinks. "I do whatever the fuck I want. I'm just telling you he's a huge asshole so you should save yourself the heartache."

"Thanks for the tip, but he already broke my heart."

Misty smiles like it's the funniest thing she's ever said in her life and it fucking kills me. She meets my eyes. "You ready to go?"

I nod because I can't get over any of it—not the fact that Silvie is trying to ruin this for me, not the fact that Misty looks like a fucking supermodel, and definitely not the fact that at least tonight, she's going to be on my arm. I lick my lips and offer her my hand to take.

"Wow," Silvie says, shaking her head. "Just wow."

"Please leave it alone," I say as I squeeze Misty's hand in mine and we walk past her.

"You are a literal piece of shit," she says loudly. "I regret wasting any of my time with you."

She's still screaming after me as we get in the elevator and take it down to the lobby.

"Sorry about that," I say.

"It's fine." Misty takes her hand out of mine and I shut my eyes momentarily.

"It's not."

"I'm no one to judge," she says as we step out into the lobby and head to the door. "You should definitely reconsider the way you treat women though."

"The way I treat women?" I let out a laugh. "I treat women exceptionally well."

"Yep, and it shows from the little scene I just witnessed."

She shoots me a look as we walk outside and I open the door of my car for her.

"I was always nice to her," I say as I get into the driver's seat and turn on the car. "I broke things off and she can't seem to accept it."

"Maybe you shouldn't have given her hope. She obviously thought there was room for more in your relationship."

"What relationship? We didn't have a relationship." I shake my head as I drive to the restaurant.

"Some people would say we didn't have a relationship either," she says. "I mean, two whole months? Does that even count?"

"Stop." I glance at her as I turn onto the street and park the car in front of the valet. "Do not compare what we had to me and Silvie."

We get out of the car and I hand over my keys to the valet, who recognizes me and asks for a selfie. Even though I'm wound up from my conversation, I oblige and smile for the camera, as I always do.

"I guess you better get used to that," Misty says when I reach her.

I don't respond. Instead, I open the door to the restaurant, greet the hostess, and let her know we have a reservation. Thankfully, even though I know she also wants to say something from the way her eyes light up, she doesn't and just seats us immediately. Maybe I have a don't-fuck-with-me look on my face now. I hope I do. I want to sit down and set-tle this as quickly as possible. We sit, grab our menus, and look through them. I set mine down.

"What we had was real," I say, staring at Misty's menu, since she's covering her entire body with it.

"Sure, but some people would say it isn't. You were messing around with that girl for over a year." She lowers the menu and leans forward, lowering her voice. "You were fucking her for over a year. That's a long time. A lot longer than you were fucking me."

I flinch. "Misty."

"It's true. I fucked guys longer than we were together as well." Her eyes narrow. "How does that make you feel?"

"Not good." I shut my eyes, wishing she'd take all of that back, but I know she won't. I open my eyes and swal-low. "I hate that."

"Yeah, well, welcome to my world. And still you think we can make this work. I just . . . " She shakes her head, lean-ing back in her chair and going back to the menu. "What the fuck is the point anyway?"

"The point is to be together."

"Together." She laughs. "What will happen when you get drafted?"

"We'll figure it out."

"We'll figure it out." She shakes her head. "The draft is soon."

"I know."

"What round will you go, do you know?"

"First."

"You seem pretty sure about that." She raises an eyebrow.

"I'm absolutely sure. If that wasn't the case, I wouldn't have gone to college at all."

"Explain something to me." She lowers the menu again and leans forward. I do the same, wishing this table was smaller so that I could be all up in her space. "Why would you want to get into a relationship now, when you're about to become rich and famous and women are going to be throwing themselves all over you? It sounds like a recipe for disaster."

"It's not."

"Explain." She taps her fingers on the table, waiting. The server interrupts us and we put in our orders quickly. When we finish, Misty is still staring at me.

"Women already throw themselves all over me. They have for . . . the majority of my life. This isn't new territory to me. I can have whoever I want, but the only person I actually want is sitting across from me right now."

"Why? When did you figure out that I'm the one you want."

"I always knew."

"Yet you were busy fucking women like Silvie and leading them on."

"Jesus." I rub my hands over my face.

"Why not have a relationship with someone? It doesn't make any sense. All these years and you never had a girlfriend."

"I told you, baseball was my number one priority."

"It still is, clearly, so what changed?"

"You're not making this easy, Misty."

"Am I supposed to? Do you expect me to flail all over you because you're hot and are about to get a fat paycheck?"

"No."

"Is that why you want me? Because I don't need you?"

"That's one of the reasons."

"Give me another reason."

"You're smart. You're beautiful. You're funny. You're an asshole."

"Oh, so we're openly admitting we like assholes now?" She tries to fight a smile, but fails.

"You did call me an asshole earlier."

"I hated you for such a long time," she says, her words nearly a whisper. "And I realize that was on me. I couldn't make you love me."

"I did though." I put my hand over hers. "I did love you."

"You didn't say that."

"What was I supposed to say? I wanted you to leave and not look back. I didn't want to hurt you."

"But you did and you made me feel like my feelings were invalid."

"I'm so sorry." I squeeze her hand.

"Stop apologizing." She takes her hand from underneath mine.

"What can I do for you to give me a chance?"

"Keep showing up."

"That simple?" I try not to smile, but it's useless; this is the most hope she's given me in years.

"That simple."

"So you'll officially date me?" I'm full-on smiling now, and I don't even care.

"Let's not go that far. I didn't agree to that."

"But you'll go on dates with me and not see other guys?"

"Are you going to see other girls?"

"No. Hell no. I haven't been with anyone all year."

"Not even Silvie?"

"Especially not Silvie." I chuckle, then get serious again. "I'm going to take you out every night this week and next week and the one after that until you choose me."

"Okay." She smiles and my heart booms.

Chapter Thirty-Two

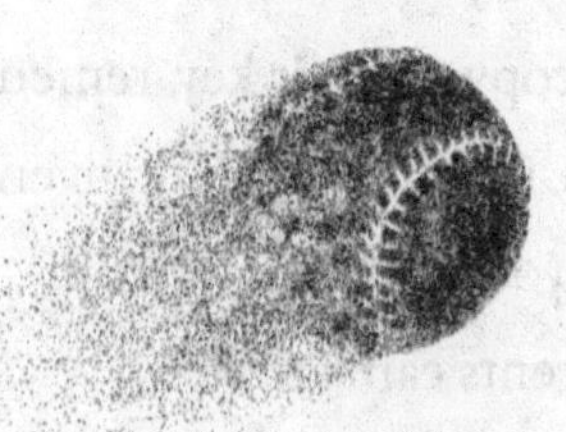

Misty

MITCHELL WASN'T KIDDING ABOUT SEEING ME EVERY DAY, though we haven't exactly gone on actual dates or had much fun. I've been working on the article, finally, and working, and he's been busy with practice, so we've seen each other maybe for ten minutes here and there. He's also had Maverick over every night, so that hasn't worked out in our favor either. Somehow, those stolen moments have made things even sweeter. A kiss before class or work. Some heavy petting that never leads where we want it to since someone always needs him for something. It's frustrating, but it's a nice change and it reminds me so much of when we first got together. That entire first month had been about flirting and kissing and pushing limits. A noise wakes me and I look at the clock to see it's three thirty in the morning. I sit up quickly, heart pounding when I hear the sound of footsteps.

"Misty."

"Mitch?" I rub my eyes. "What the—"

"You gave me a copy of your key, remember?"

"Yeah." I frown in the dark. I'd given him the key three days ago. "And you never showed up."

"Because my parents came over."

"Oh." My frown deepens. "I didn't even know they were in town."

"You've been busy." He walks up to my bed and sits beside me.

"It's almost four in the morning." I yawn. "Don't tell me you're here to take me on a jog because I swear I'll scream."

He chuckles. "I wouldn't dream of it."

"Then what—"

He stops my question with a kiss. A hard kiss against my lips that pushes all thoughts out of my head. His tongue slips into my mouth and his hands start working their way down my body. I sit up to assist him in taking off my clothes, and then help him with his. He takes a step back and looks at me. I can't see much of him, only shadows, but I can definitely see his cock, hard and ready. He leans down, pulling me into a kiss again, as his hand reaches between my legs, finding my clit.

"Oh my God," I whisper against his mouth.

He takes his hand away and I whimper at the loss of contact. He moves onto the bed and grabs my waist, guiding me over him. I begin to settle over his hard-on, but he continues to move me higher.

"Sit on my face," he says, his voice so low it's almost a groan, as if he can't take it anymore. I do as I'm told and shiver at the first lick over my clit. "Move, baby," he commands, but he's the one gripping my ass, making sure I move over his tongue. He's no longer teasing, but sucking my clit and licking my folds, and when he reaches up to roll my nipples with his fingers, I feel my entire body go hot and cold, and start to come on his mouth.

Mitch doesn't give me a chance to fully come down from the orgasm before he tosses me on my back and starts pumping his fingers inside of me.

"Fuck," is all I can manage. Groans and pleads and mewls as he takes what he wants or gives me what I want, the two are entwined in each other now. His fingers work my clit and inside, and my eyes roll and my back arches and I can't help but orgasming again. This time, I don't wait. I sit up and push him back against the headboard and sit on him.

"Holy shit." He hisses as I take him in completely and begin to ride him hard and fast. "Fuck, Misty. Fuck."

"God, you feel good," I moan.

"You were made for me," he says, and catches my eye as he palms my breasts, his expression hazy with lust, echoing my own. "You were fucking made for me."

I keep rocking against him, feeling the familiar pressure build as he pumps into me. His body tenses against mine and I know he's close. I pick up the pace, throwing my head back, feeling every inch of him hitting me inside as his fingers find my clit again. My knees begin to shake, my entire body seems to buckle over him, and then I come. He flips me around quickly and pulls out, coming on me, the warm, sticky liquid hitting my breasts, my stomach, my chin. I hold his gaze as he marks me, and I feel myself crack open for him once more. He climbs out of bed and brings back a wet towel to clean me with, helping me get up and leading me to the bathroom. Our eyes meet in the mirror and I feel my heart explode. As if feeling the same, he turns me to face him and kisses me deeply. When he pulls away, he exhales and looks at me for a long moment.

"I love you." He swallows. "I should have said that to you five years ago. I've loved you since then. That's why this is going to work this time. I've been holding out for you."

"You've been holding out for me?" I raise an eyebrow.

"My heart, babe. My heart is yours."

"And your body." I run a finger down his chiseled torso.

"Fuck yes." He kisses me again, then carries me back to bed.

Chapter Thirty-Three

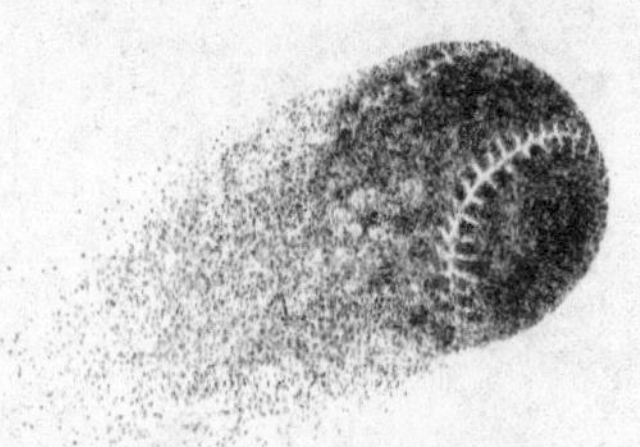

Misty

TAKE A DEEP BREATH AND LET IT OUT AS I WAIT FOR VALERIE'S feedback on my article. She's been reading it slowly, as if analyzing every single word and it's making me feel like I need to throw up. In high school, I was the editor of my newspaper and in charge of yearbook. At Duke, I quickly joined the newspaper team and have written more articles than I can count. Yet, none have been more important than this one. Judging by Mitch and his teammates reactions to it when I let them read it last week, I know I did the players justice.

"This is good." Valerie looks up from the screen and takes off her reading glasses.

"Thanks." I wring my hands together on my lap. "I stuck to the facts."

"You paint the athletes in a really good light. You don't even name the ones arrested for selling drugs."

"Well, I didn't think it was important. These athletes live and breathe their sport and don't have an opportunity to make money, so most of them are jobless. If a man who's seemingly rich offers them an opportunity to make easy money, why wouldn't they take it?"

"I agree." Valerie nods. "This is a fair and deep analysis to the issues colleges need to look at. It's brilliant, Misty."

"You really think so?" I hold my breath, because even though I know she liked it, I feel like I still have so much learning and growing to do.

"I know so."

"Do you think you'll publish it?" I bite my lip, knee bouncing as I wait for her to confirm or deny this.

"I mean . . ." she turns the computer screen to face me and I see a photograph of Mitch and some of his teammates wearing their uniforms and looking at the camera. They're all serious, like they mean business. My heart skips a beat at the sight of Mitch. It skips another when I read the bottom of the cover. *College Sports – Professionals or Not? By Misty Canó*

I bring my attention back to Valerie. "This is real?"

"I mean, the title may change, but yes, this is real." She smiles. "Congratulations, Misty. You should be receiving an A in the class and a front page debut in our magazine."

"Oh my . . . " I whisper. "Can I buy a copy?"

"You'll be provided a few copies. I'll give you an unfinished one right now." She winks. "Go celebrate."

I walk out of the building feeling like I'm walking on a cloud. Mitch is standing outside of his car, practicing his pitching with no ball and no mound. It's something he does constantly. There isn't a moment when he's not talking about or practicing his sport. I find myself both amused and in awe of his determination. Mitch was the one who sat quietly in bed beside me as I finished this article. He was the one who kept telling me I could do it, even when that blank page and blinking curser on my screen felt like an impossibility. When I get closer, he stops pitching and closes the distance between us.

"How'd it go?"

I wave the pages in my hand, tears filling my eyes.

"They're publishing it?" He grins wide, rushing over now, opening his arms for me and wrapping them so tightly around me that I think I may just break. "They're publishing it."

"They're publishing it," I say between tears. He sets me down and wipes them with his thumbs, crashing his lips against mine and pulling away to search my eyes.

"Are you happy?"

"So happy." I laugh, new tears spilling. "Look."

He takes the unfinished magazine from my hands, the magazine his parents own, and even though that would normally have made me think this was given to me, I know better than that. I worked for this. I wrote an incredible article. I followed these guys who became my family and this one in particular whom I proudly call my boyfriend. I did this. Mitchell looks at the magazine in his hands, shaking his head like he can't believe it.

"I'm so proud of you," he says, glancing at me. "So proud, baby."

"Thank you." I wipe my tears. "I dedicated it to someone."

"Really?" He goes through it and stops when he reaches the beginning of the article. I watch his eyes as they move over the words, and his smile when he's done reading it. He shakes his head again and looks up at me. "My girlfriend is a legit journalist."

"Very legit." I smile wide.

"This means so much to me. To all of us, but to me especially." He hugs me close again. "Thank you for telling the world how hard we work."

"You show them that every season. I just stated the facts." I kiss his jaw.

"Hm." He pulls away slightly once more and this time,

when he kisses me, I feel my toes curl and my entire body ignite. "Let's go celebrate this."

"Let's celebrate." I squeal when he lifts me into his arms and carries me to the car.

I tighten my arms around his neck and lay against his chest. There's no one else I'd rather be celebrating with than this man.

Chapter Thirty-Four

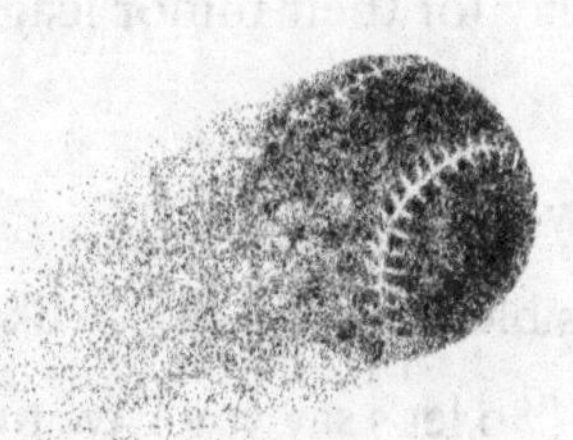

Mitchell

"YOU SAID YOU HAVE QUESTIONS. WHAT ARE THEY?" My knee bounces as I wait.

I brought Misty to a little bar on Franklin and asked for a seat in the back to make sure we wouldn't be disturbed. Of course, having this conversation at her apartment or mine would have been better for privacy, but I didn't want to risk either one of us getting up in the middle of the conversation. Ever since we came out to our parents and siblings that we were together, it's been one thing after another. Celebrations on all sides, but with those celebrations come questions – are you moving in together? Are you getting engaged? Do you both want kids? As if finishing school and getting drafted by a major league team isn't enough, they've added a load of questions on our plates. I'm okay with all of it. My answer to everything having to do with Misty is yes, but I can tell she's overwhelmed.

"What happens after you get drafted?" she asks.

"Most likely, I play for their minor league team until they move me up."

She frowns. "So you can't just start?"

"Anything is possible, but that's more likely."

She nods slowly. "So let's say you have to go live in like Missouri for a year or two . . . am I supposed to go live in Missouri as well?"

"Why Missouri?" I chuckle. "Of all the teams, how'd you come up with that one?"

"Oh. I don't know." She smiles. "I was trying to think of a place I'd never been before and Missouri fit the bill."

"Well, I'd be traveling a lot. One hundred and forty-four games a year." I raise an eyebrow at her. "So, I guess that would be up to you."

"That is a lot of games." She chews her bottom lip and looks away.

My heart pounds. There's absolutely nothing I want more than to have her by my side all the time. As much as possible. I know how that number sounds though. It's a lot of games and a lot of travel and Misty is independent and has her own career to think about.

"I'm not getting drafted by the Cardinals, Mist." I reach for her hand. "I mean, I might, but most likely I'll go to the Mets or Yankees, and that would mean moving to New York. Well, the Mets minor league plays in Florida, but like I said, I'm not anticipating being in the minors very long."

"I want to go where you go." She squeezes my hand. "I really do, but I don't want to be one of those people who puts her own things on hold for her boyfriend and then something happens and we break up and I never get it back, you know?"

"We're not going to break up. Not ever." I shoot her a pointed look. "I mean that. I would never jeopardize this. And you're right, I don't want you to put your own things on hold. I want you to do whatever you want, which is why I'm not pushing this. And we don't even know what's going to happen yet."

"So maybe we should wait and see?"

"We can have this conversation again in three months." I wink.

She blushes. "I hate when you wink at me in public."

"Why's that?" I grin.

"You know why."

"Because you want to jump my bones but can't?"

"Exactly." She licks her lips slowly. My cock hardens instantly.

I put my hand up to call the waitress' attention. "I'm paying and then we're going straight to your place."

"Good." She laughs, then looks at her watch. "I have two hours before I need to be at the coffee shop."

"I only need one."

Misty laughs again and I feel myself smile. We'll have this conversation again in three months, and by then, I'll have my own question for her.

Epilogue

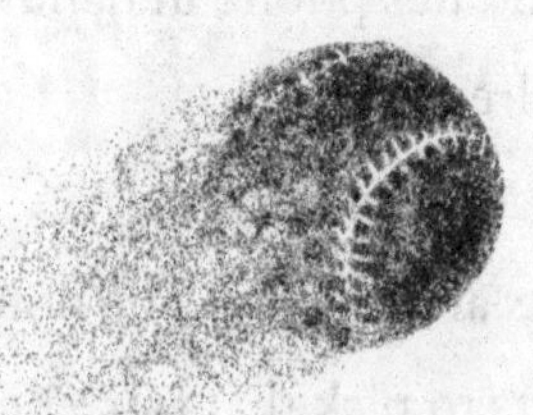

3 months later

"HOW DOES THIS WORK?" MY KNEE WON'T QUIT BOUNCING. "When will this guy start talking?"

We're in The Cruzes' New York penthouse, waiting for Mitch and his agent to finish their meeting. They've been with Mitch's father in his home office for an hour now and I don't know if my anxiety can handle any more of this waiting.

"Don't you have something you can smoke to help you calm down?" Jagger asks with a laugh.

"Hilarious. I stopped smoking. I took two Ashwa gummies and they don't seem to be working."

"We're out of wine, so cheese, crackers, salami, and water it is," Milly Cruz says, walking in with the second charcuterie board of the day. The guys ate everything on the first one.

"Thank you." I smile, reaching for a cracker and cheese before these guys clear this out as well.

"There's a leak in the clinic. Thankfully I have someone who can take care of it while we're here," Jo says, walking in with a magazine and her phone in hand. "I am so ready for this honeymoon already."

"Did you book?" Milly asks.

"The plane tickets are booked. The hotels are to be determined. Jagger wants to pick that since he didn't help me do anything for the wedding." Jo's lips twist.

"The wedding was perfect," Milly says.

"Best pink wedding ever," I say, smiling.

They had a super intimate wedding last month right here in New York. It was only family and a few friends. I'd always thought Jo would have an elaborate wedding, but it turns out, small weddings are so much better. She wasn't stressed about anything, and she had so much fun and was so happy. I don't think I ever want to get married, but if I did, I'd follow in her footsteps. It's something Mitch and I agree on. We'd rather just live together and not worry about a legally binding contract. Though, now that the cat is out of the bag and everyone knows we're dating, that's the number one question everyone asks: *when are you getting married?*

The doorbell rings and Milly jumps. "That must be your parents."

My parents, who are also in town this weekend for the occasion. Rocky's parents are also on their way. Mitch's draft watch party has somehow become a bigger thing than Jagger and Jo's entire wedding. Milly says in the past, we would have gone somewhere for the occasion, there would have been a stage and cheers, but Mitch didn't want to leave anyone behind. He wanted both his brothers and their spouses, and the in-laws, to all be there with him, and so, we ended up here.

Both sets of parents arrive back-to-back and the greetings are loud, to say the least. Mom walks in with a crate of wine, Rocky's mom walks in with platters of food that smell heavenly and we all jump up to see what's in them. There's a cameraman here, provided by the television network, to record us as we watch the actual draft, and even he's eyeing the food now.

"Patties with coco bread," Mav shouts. "Best in-laws ever."

"Save me one," I shout back.

"Did someone say Jamaican patties?" Mitch asks walking over, huge grin on his face. My heart stops when his eyes meet mine.

"What happened?"

"Turn up the television," his dad says, voice booming.

I run back to the TV and shakily unmute it, my eyes bouncing between the guy on the screen and Mitchell, who's all nonchalant, smiling like the freaking Cheshire Cat. There are two men on ESPN talking about Mitch and showing his college highlights, saying he could definitely be in the lineup if the Yankees wanted him to be there right now. Another one responds that he agrees, but that either way it won't take him very long to get up to the big leagues anyway. Their conversation is cut to another man standing behind a podium.

"With the first pick of the 2021 draft, the New York Yankees select Mitchell Cruz, a pitcher from the University of North Carolina."

A high-pitched scream echoes through the penthouse, all of us jumping and cheering, and I realize that I'm full-on crying when I turn to Mitchell, who's hugging his parents before he looks for me and walks over as his brothers jump, patting him on the back. He grabs ahold of my face and wipes my tears with his thumbs as I laugh.

"You did it," I say, laughing, tears still streaming down my face.

"With you, anything is possible." He kisses me then, and I forget about everyone in the room. I wrap my arms around him and kiss him harder, pulling him closer.

On the television, they're showing more of his highlights and comparing him to his father, as they often do, but

Mitchell seems unbothered, his attention is all on me. He pulls away slightly and kneels down. My heart stops beating.

"Mitch."

"I know we said we didn't care about getting married, but I lied." He grins, opening a box with a huge diamond ring. "Will you marry me, Misty?"

I'm crying harder as I nod rapidly. As he slips the ring on my finger and stands up to kiss me, I hear myself say yes loudly, the sound coming from the television. I glance over to see that the cameraman has caught it all on camera and they're airing our proposal for the world to see.

"Oh my God. Look at my hair." I start fixing the loose strands and everyone laughs, including the commentators.

The camera cuts from us and they keep talking, now about the proposal, no longer about Mitch and his dad, and as we celebrate with our families, in the same penthouse we once were together in when we were teenagers, I don't think I can get any happier.

"Best day of my life," Mitch says, kissing me. "Best day of my entire fucking life."

I couldn't agree more.

ClaireContrerasbooks.com

Twitter:
@ClariCon

Insta:
ClaireContreras

Facebook:
www.facebook.com/groups/ClaireContrerasBooks

Other Books

The Heart Series

Kaleidoscope Hearts

Torn Hearts

Paper Hearts

Elastic Hearts

Darkness Series

There is No Light in Darkness

Darkness Before Dawn